MODERN HUMANITIES RESEARCH ASSOCIATION
NEW TRANSLATIONS
VOLUME 20

MIDNIGHT

MHRA NEW TRANSLATIONS

The guiding principle of this series is to publish new translations into English of important works that have been hitherto imperfectly translated or that are entirely untranslated. The work to be translated or re-translated should be aesthetically or intellectually important. Proposals for new entries in the series are welcome. The proposal should cover such issues as copyright and, where relevant, an account of the faults of the previous translation/s; it should be accompanied by independent statements from two experts in the field attesting to the significance of the original work (in cases where this is not obvious) and to the desirability of a new or renewed translation.

Translations should be accompanied by a fairly substantial intro-duction and other, briefer, apparatus: a note on the translation; a select bibliography; a chronology of the author's life and works; and notes to the text.

Titles are selected by members of the Editorial Board and edited by leading academics.

General Editor

Dr Ann Lewis

Editorial Board

Dr Ann Lewis (French)
Professor Ritchie Robertson (Germanic)
Professor Helena Sanson (Italian)
Professor Cláudia Pazos Alonso (Portuguese)
Professor David Gillespie (Slavonic)
Professor Jonathan Thacker (Spanish)

texts.mhra.org.uk

MIDNIGHT
ASTRAL VISION OF A MOMENT OF WAR

By
RAMÓN MARÍA DEL VALLE-INCLÁN

Translated by
ELIZABETH DRUMM

MODERN HUMANITIES RESEARCH ASSOCIATION
New Translations 20
2025

Published by

The Modern Humanities Research Association

Salisbury House
Station Road
Cambridge CB1 2LA
United Kingdom

First published 2025

ISBN 978-1-83954-604-4 (hardback)
ISBN 978-1-83954-605-1 (paperback)
ISBN 978-1-83954-606-8 (ebook)

Set in Minion 3

CONTENTS

List of Figures   vi

Acknowledgements   vii

Introduction   1

    Ramón del Valle-Inclán: Life and Work   3

    Valle-Inclán at the Western Front: The 'Notebook from France'   10

    A Theory behind Astral Vision: *The Lamp of Marvels*   19

    Valle-Inclán's Disclaimer: 'I Have Failed in my Resolve'   25

    Astral Vision and Ethical Action   29

Translator's Note   35

Midnight: Astral Vision of a Moment of War   37

Bibliography   75

FIGURES

FIG. 1. Title page from *La media noche* (1917)   viii

FIG. 2. Map indicating location of place names
referenced in *Midnight*   12

FIG. 3. Opening of Chapter 1 from *La media noche* (1917)   38

ACKNOWLEDGEMENTS

My THANKS to Reed College colleagues Sharon Larisch and Nathalia King, and to Beth Muench, for their careful reading of the manuscript, to Margarita Santos Zas and other scholars from the Grupo de Investigación Valle-Inclán at the Universidad de Santiago de Compostela for insightful orientation, and to my husband, John Muench, enthusiastic traveller and constant source of support and encouragement. I gratefully acknowledge that this translation has been made possible, in part, by a grant from the National Endowment for the Humanities. Excerpts of the translation originally appeared in Ramón del Valle-Inclán, '*Midnight: Astral Vision of a Moment of War* (Excerpts)', trans. by Elizabeth Drumm, *PMLA*, 136.3 (2021), pp. 401–16, published by the Modern Language Association of America.

LA MEDIA NOCHE
VISIÓN ESTELAR DE VN
MOMENTO DE GVERRA
POR DON RAMÓN DEL
VALLE-INCLÁN

MADRID, MCMXVII

FIG. 1. Title page from *La media noche* (Imprenta Clásica Española, 1917). Image courtesy of *Cátedra Valle-Inclán*.

INTRODUCTION

THE EARLY twentieth-century Spanish author Ramón del Valle-Inclán (1866–1936) was a remarkable innovator who wrote poetry, novels, theatre, essays, and art criticism. His works experimented with the transgeneric potential of literary form and included a series of four literary sonatas; a trilogy of 'savage comedies'; and the *esperpentos* (monstrosities), a genre he created to express the grotesque tragedy that characterized his contemporary Spain. Renowned for a (fictionalized) duel in which he lost an arm, as well as for his long beard, nineteenth-century cape, and other features of a carefully curated public persona, Valle-Inclán was a legendary figure in Madrid and his native Galicia.

Valle-Inclán visited the Western Front in 1916 at the invitation of the French government. He recorded his experiences in a notebook, published in facsimile by the University of Santiago de Compostela in 2016 as *El cuaderno de Francia* ('Notebook from France').[1] The notes were a source for a fictionalized chronicle published as *Un día de guerra (visión estelar)* ('A Day at War (Astral Vision)') between October 1916 and February 1917 in the Madrid newspaper *El Imparcial*. The short novel translated here represents a substantial rewriting of this newspaper account. Published in April 1917, *La media noche: visión estelar de un momento de guerra* (*Midnight: Astral Vision of a Moment of War*) augments the number of chapters that comprise the serialized version from thirty-four to forty and, importantly, adds an introductory 'Breve noticia' ('Brief Notice'), in which Valle-Inclán introduces central problems of time and perspective, explicitly tying the chronicle to his aesthetic treatise of 1916, *La lámpara maravillosa: ejercicios espirituales* (*The Lamp of Marvels: Aesthetic Meditations*).[2] As we will see in a later

1 Ramón del Valle-Inclán, *Con el alba: el cuaderno de Francia (1916). Manuscrito inédito de Ramón del Valle-Inclán*, ed. by Margarita Santos Zas, facsimile edn (Universidade de Santiago de Compostela, 2016). Further references to this text are indicated parenthetically by 'Notebook' and the page number. Unless otherwise indicated, all translations from Spanish are my own.

2 Ramón del Valle-Inclán, *Un día de guerra (visión estelar) — La media noche:*

section of this introduction, if the aesthetic treatise represents a consolidation of concepts Valle-Inclán had been developing over the previous decade, the novel *Midnight: Astral Vision of a Moment of War* puts these concepts into practice.³ The treatise and novel together are a remarkable example of a unique, early twentieth-century Spanish response to aesthetic concerns of literary modernists across Europe and the Americas, including the desire to disengage qualitative experience from its fragmentary expression in language, to express discrete temporalities as simultaneous, and to observe perspectival space from a position of cosmic omniscience.⁴

It is difficult to pinpoint a cause for Valle-Inclán's relative lack of recognition outside of Spain. Certainly, censorship during the dictatorship of Francisco Franco (1939–1975) had a devastating effect on the circulation of the work of Republican authors who were thriving in the 1920s and early 1930s.⁵ During the war and long years of the dictatorship,

visión estelar de un momento de guerra, ed. by Bénédicte Vauthier and Margarita Santos Zas, 3 vols (Universidade de Santiago de Compostela, 2017); Ramón del Valle-Inclán, *La lámpara maravillosa: ejercicios espirituales*, ed. by Francisco Javier Blasco Pascual (Espasa Calpe, 1995). All translations into English of *La lámpara maravillosa* are from Ramón del Valle-Inclán, *The Lamp of Marvels: Aesthetic Meditations*, trans. by Robert Lima (Lindisfarne Press, 1986). Further references to the English translation are indicated parenthetically in the text. The original edition of *La media noche* (Imprenta Clásica Española, 1917) was richly decorated with woodcuts by José Moya del Pino (1891–1969); it is accessible online, courtesy of the *Cátedra Valle-Inclán*, <https://www.cervantesvirtual.com/obra/la-media-noche-vision-estelar-de-un-momento-de-guerra-875777>.

3 The numerous precursor texts of *La lámpara maravillosa* are presented in Carmen E. Vílchez Ruiz, 'De las ideas estéticas de Valle-Inclán en la prensa periódica (1902–1916): armonía de contrarios', in *Literatura hispánica y prensa periódica (1875–1931): actas del Congreso Internacional, Lugo, 25–28 de noviembre 2008*, ed. by Javier Serrano Alonso and Amparo de Juan Bolufer (Universidade de Santiago de Compostela, 2009), pp. 637–48. Quotations from *Midnight: Astral Vision of a Moment of War* in this introduction are cited parenthetically; the page numbers refer to the present edition.

4 For further discussion of these and other aspects of Valle-Inclán's narrative innovation in *Midnight*, see Dru Dougherty, 'Valle-Inclán, corresponsal de guerra: *La media noche*', in *Literatura hispánica*, ed. by Alonso and Juan Bolufer, pp. 565–85; Valle-Inclán, *Un día de guerra*, I, pp. 89–159; and Darío Villanueva, '*La media noche* de Valle-Inclán: análisis y suerte de su técnica narrativa', in *Suma Valleinclaniana*, ed. by John P. Gabriele (Anthropos, 1992), pp. 415–44.

5 Gayle Rogers, 'Jiménez, Modernism/o, and the Languages of Comparative Modernist Studies', *Comparative Literature*, 66.1 (2014), pp. 127–47; C. Christopher Soufas, Jr, 'Spain', in *The Cambridge Companion to European Modernism*, ed. by

these authors were uprooted by exile or faced imprisonment or violent death. Although Valle-Inclán died of natural causes, his work, like that of many modernist authors, was censored within Spain. Further, because of a lack of translations, Valle-Inclán and others of his generation are relatively unknown outside of Spain, a situation which results in, among other effects, the lack of a critical tradition that would put them in conversation with literary modernists of other traditions.[6] Valle-Inclán's interest in time, perspectivism, and other literary questions from the period is shared across these traditions, but as we will see, astral vision, and the particular internal dialogism that this perspectivism creates, is his unique contribution.

Ramón del Valle-Inclán: Life and Work

Ramón del Valle-Inclán was born in 1866 in Vilanova de Arousa, a small town in Galicia, a region in the north-west of Spain. His father was a journalist and champion of Republican causes, including Galician autonomy, and relatives on his mother's side were traditional, conservative members of the aristocracy, a cultural inheritance that finds expression in several of Valle-Inclán's early works set in Galicia.[7] While

Pericles Lewis (Cambridge University Press, 2011), pp. 151–69; and José Manuel Pereiro Otero, *La escritura modernista de Valle-Inclán: orgía de colores* (Verbum, 2008), discuss the effect of censorship and exile on authors from the period.

6 For studies which address the relative isolation of Spanish modernist authors within the larger context see Mary Lee Bretz, *Encounters Across Borders: The Changing Visions of Spanish Modernism, 1890–1930* (Bucknell University Press, 2001); Darío Villanueva, *Valle-Inclán, novelista del modernism* (Editorial Tirant lo Blanch, 2005); Jessica Schiff Berman, *Modernist Commitments: Ethics, Politics, and Transnational Modernism* (Columbia University Press, 2011); and Gayle Rogers, *Modernism and the New Spain: Britain, Cosmopolitan Europe, and Literary History* (Oxford University Press, 2012).

7 For a full biography of Ramón del Valle-Inclán, along with digitized copies of his works, bibliography, and other information compiled by the Grupo de Investigación Valle-Inclán at the University of Santiago de Compostela see *Cátedra Valle-Inclán*, ed. by Margarita Santos Zas and others (Centro de Humanidades Digitales de la Universidad de Alicante, 2008) <https://www.cervantesvirtual.com/portales/catedra_valle_inclan/presentacion> [accessed 12 December 2024]. The Grupo de Investigación Valle-Inclán maintains the *Archivo digital Valle-Inclán*, a database with over 3750 documents and over 70,000 images: Carmen E. Vílchez Ruiz and others (eds), *Archivo digital Valle-Inclán (1888–1936)* (Universidade de Santiago de Compostela, 2018) <https://www.archivodigitalvalleinclan.es> [accessed 12 December 2024].

studying law at the University of Santiago de Compostela, Valle-Inclán began publishing poetry and short stories in the press. He also immersed himself in various occult practices in vogue at the time, including spiritism and theosophy.[8] He abandoned his university studies in 1889, and in 1892 travelled to Mexico, collaborating with newspapers in Mexico City and Veracruz. This first experience in the Americas impacted Valle-Inclán greatly, putting him in contact with leading authors like the poet Rubén Darío and with trends in Latin American modernism.[9] In 1921 he remarked about this early experience that 'México me abrió los ojos y me hizo poeta' ('Mexico opened my eyes and made me a poet').[10]

In 1895, Valle-Inclán moved to Madrid and participated actively in the capital's cultural scene, publishing his first book, *Femeninas: seis historias amorosas* ('Femininities: Six Love Stories', 1895), a collection of short stories influenced by the literary decadentism in vogue at the time. He famously presided over a *tertulia* ('café conversation') at the Nuevo Café de Levante from 1903 to 1916 that included important authors like Darío, Antonio Machado, and Pío Baroja as well as leading visual artists, including Santiago Rusiñol, Julio Romero de Torres, and José Gutiérrez Solana.[11] The ongoing exchange of ideas among artists, intellectuals, and literary figures encouraged by Madrid's vibrant *tertulia*

8 Eliphas Lévi (1810–1875) coined the term *occult* to describe practices concerned with 'analogies and equilibrations between visible and invisible worlds'. See n. 17 to this introduction for context regarding the practice of theosophy in Spain. Virginia Garlitz, 'El ocultismo finisecular en Valle-Inclán', *El Pasajero*, 22 (2013) <https://www.elpasajero.com/ventolera/garlitzoccultismesp.html> [accessed 5 June 2023].

9 The Spanish term *modernismo*, defined more narrowly than its European counterpart, established temporal and geographic boundaries for the movement that do not line up with those of European modernism. Gayle Rogers explains that the term coalesced first in Latin America during the 1890s around the poetry of Nicaraguan author Rubén Darío. The Latin American modernist movement made its way to Spain in the early decades of the twentieth century and lost influence with the death of Darío in 1916 and the rise of various Spanish avant-garde movements (Rogers, 'Jiménez', p. 129). For further discussion, see Bretz, *Encounters Across Borders*, pp. 13–69; and C. Christopher Soufas, Jr, *The Subject in Question: Early Contemporary Spanish Literature and Modernism* (Catholic University of America Press, 2007), pp. 1–18.

10 Cited in Santos Zas, 'Introducción a la vida y obra de Valle-Inclán', in *Cátedra Valle-Inclán* <https://www.cervantesvirtual.com/portales/catedra_valle_inclan/vida_primeras_publicaciones> [accessed 10 March 2025].

11 Margarita Santos Zas, 'Valle-Inclán, contertulio: el nuevo café de levante', *Insula: revista de letras y ciencias humanas*, 738 (2008), pp. 13–15.

culture contributed greatly to Valle-Inclán's richly visual literary practice — his painterly vision — and, in general, was vitally important to the
consolidation of modernism in Spain.[12] In 1908 and 1912, Valle-Inclán
wrote two series of articles about the national Exposición de Bellas Artes
('Fine Art Exposition') of those years in which he presented works by
Romero de Torres and Rusiñol, among others, as well as several aesthetic concepts like the harmony of opposites or memory as the site of
what is real, which eventually found their way into the aesthetic treatise
The Lamp of Marvels.[13]

Valle-Inclán's published literary work from this period exemplifies
anti-realist, modernist trends from the turn of the century: intertextual and interartistic references, experimental use of synaesthesia, and
the rhythmic prose that became a hallmark of Valle-Inclán's writing
throughout his long career. Four literary sonatas, for example, published in successive years beginning in 1902, record in memoir form the
amorous adventures of the Marquis de Bradomín, a Galician aristocrat
memorably self-characterized in a triad of adjectives as 'feo, católico, y

---

12 Serge Salaün, 'Valle-Inclán y la pintura', *Hecho teatral: revista de teoría y práctica del teatro hispánico*, 1 (2001), pp. 115–35. The article introduces Valle-Incan's
'cultura pictórica enciclopédica' ('encyclopedic pictorial culture') and identifies
several influences from the plastic arts in Valle-Inclán's literary texts. Attesting to
his lifelong interest in the plastic arts, Valle-Inclán was a professor of aesthetics at
the Escuela de Pintura, Escultura, y Grabado (School for Painting, Sculpture, and
Etching) from 1916 to 1919, and held two appointments during the Second Spanish
Republic from 1931 to 1936: Conservador del Patrimonio Artístico Nacional y
Director del Museo de Aranjuez (Conservator of the National Artistic Patrimony
and Director of the Aranjuez Museum) and Director of the Fine Arts Academy in
Rome.

13 Ramón del Valle-Inclán, *Obras completas*, ed. by Margarita Santos Zas and others, 5 vols (Fundación José Antonio de Castro, 2018), II, pp. 1494–1512, 1557–64.
There are ten essays concerning the exposition of 1908 and four concerning that
of 1912. Concepts introduced in the essays that are incorporated into *La lámpara
maravillosa* have been discussed in Elizabeth Drumm, 'La estética del recuerdo en
La lámpara maravillosa: el proceso de pensar el tiempo', in *Valle-Inclán y las artes:
congreso internacional, Santiago de Compostela, 25–28 de octubre de 2011*, ed. by
Margarita Santos Zas, Javier Serrano, and Amparo de Juan Bolufer (Universidade
de Santiago de Compostela, 2012), pp. 303–20; Virigina Garlitz, *El centro del
círculo: 'La lámpara maravillosa' de Valle-Inclán* (Universidade de Santiago de
Compostela, 2007); Eliane Lavaud, 'Valle-Inclán y la Exposición de Bellas Artes de
1908', *Papeles de Son Armadans*, 81 (1976), pp. 115–28; Jean-Marie Lavaud, 'Une collaboration de Valle-Inclán au journal *Nuevo Mundo* et l'exposition de 1912', *Bulletin
Hispanique*, 71 (1969), pp. 286–311.

sentimental' ('ugly, Catholic, and sentimental'). The four sonatas are highly stylized, with each recounting escapades from a different 'season' of the life of Bradomín (the *Sonata de primavera* (*Spring Sonata*) corresponds to the youth of the narrator, the *Sonata de invierno* (*Winter Sonata*) to his old age, etc.) and each taking place in a different geographic region (Italy, Mexico, and Galicia and Navarra in Spain), evoking different settings and tones.

In 1907 Valle-Inclán married the actress Josefina Blanco, with whom he had four children. In 1910 he accompanied Blanco and the theatre company with which she was affiliated on a tour through South America, where he presented several conferences and public lectures, including, notably, one on 'Modernismo' ('Modernism') in which he again introduced several concepts that were eventually incorporated into *The Lamp of Marvels*.[14] Although the loss of his arm — the result not of a duel but, more prosaically, from an infection caused by an injury received in a barroom dispute — put to rest Valle-Inclán's early attempts at acting, he contributed to the theatre as director and dramatist. While some productions of his dramatic texts from this period were modestly successful, it is fair to conclude that Valle-Inclán's anti-realist, highly visual theatre was counter to the tastes of the Spanish theatre public in the early decades of the century. By 1912, he had given up on attempts to stage his work commercially and turned to a more experimental theatre, writing several groundbreaking dramas in the 1920s. I will return to this rich period of Valle-Inclán's literary production below but note here that although many of these dramas were not staged during Valle-Inclán's life, they pushed the boundaries of theatrical form, incorporating techniques borrowed from cinema and establishing Valle-Inclán as one of Spain's leading twentieth-century dramatists.[15]

Also important from the first decades of the twentieth century are two collections: the first two parts of the dramatic trilogy *Las comedias bárbaras* (*Savage Comedies*), set in rural Galicia and tracing the fall of Don

14 Virginia Garlitz, 'Valle-Inclán en la gira americana de 1910', in *Valle-Inclán, 1898– 1998: escenarios: seminario internacional, Universidade de Santiago de Compostela, noviembre–diciembre, 1998*, ed. by Margarita Santos Zas and others (Universidade de Santiago de Compostela, 2000), pp. 91–122. The essay 'Modernismo' is included in Valle-Inclán, *Obras completas*, II, pp. 1461–63.

15 Ramón del Valle-Inclán, *Savage Comedies*, trans. by Christopher Colbath and Luis M. González, MHRA New Translations, 15 (Modern Humanities Research Association, 2022). In their introduction, Colbath and González discuss the trilogy in terms of cinematic practice, in particular Sergei Eisenstein's montage.

Juan Manuel Montenegro, an aristocratic landowner confronted by an increasingly bourgeois, commercialized world; and the three volumes of the series *La guerra carlista* ('The Carlist War'), which use documentary sources to present a fictionalized account of the nineteenth-century wars of succession provoked by the death of King Ferdinand VII in 1833.[16] The Carlists, favouring the succession of Ferdinand's brother, don Carlos, as opposed to his daughter, the eventual Queen Isabel II, were Catholic conservatives, as opposed to the liberal, reformist proponents of Isabel II. Much has been written about Valle-Inclán's participation in the Carlist movement, often in an attempt to excuse his support for this extreme conservative cause as an aesthetic exercise. This is in part true, but it is important to note that although his political association with the Carlist party waned during and after World War I, Valle-Inclán's ideological support for the cause was documented in the press throughout his life.

In 1916, Valle-Inclán published his aesthetic treatise *The Lamp of Marvels*. Famously dismissed by the poet Juan Ramón Jiménez as a lamp that contained 'more smoke than oil', the treatise presents a dense synthesis of occult traditions as varied as Gnosticism, Neoplatonism, Spanish mysticism, Kabbalah, the Hermetic tradition, and alchemy, and it is clearly situated within the Theosophist tradition much in vogue at the beginning of the century.[17] That said, the treatise also presents a co-

16 The three works that comprise the *Savage Comedies* are *Águila de blazon* (*The Blazoned Eagle*, 1907), *Romance de lobos* (*Wolves Rampant*, 1908), and *Cara de Plata* (*Golden Boy*, 1922). The *Guerra carlista* series consists of *Los cruzados de la causa* ('Crusaders of the Cause', 1908), *El resplandor de la hoguera* ('The Bonfire's Radiance', 1909), *Gerifaltes de antaño* ('Heroes of Yesteryear', 1909), and fragments of an unfinished fourth novel, *La corte de Estella* ('The Court in Estella'), which were discovered in 1966.

17 The quote from Juan Ramón Jiménez is cited widely. See, for example, Carmen E. Vílchez Ruiz, 'La estética valleinclániana a la luz de *La lámpara maravillosa*', *Elvira: revista de estudios filológicos*, 10 (2005), pp. 89–116 (p. 102). Occult sources used by Valle-Inclán have been identified and contextualized by Virginia Garlitz and more recently by Vílchez Ruiz, who concludes that '*La lámpara maravillosa* [es] un cifrado breviario que entronca plenamente con el pensamiento teosófico finisecular' ('*The Lamp of Marvels* is an encoded breviary fully enmeshed in turn-of-the-century theosophical thought'): Carmen E. Vílchez Ruiz, 'Mística y cannabis como vía estética en Valle-Inclán: *La lámpara maravillosa*', in *Sobremesas literarias: en torno a la gastronomía en las letras Hispánicas*, ed. by Laura Peña García and Jesús Murillo Sagredo (Biblioteca Nueva, 2015), pp. 411–20 (p. 412). Theosophy was active in Spain from the 1890s, with prominent groups in Barcelona and Madrid who published several journals dedicated to transmitting

herent aesthetic system that confronts many of the philosophical problems at the heart of early twentieth-century modernism. Valle-Inclán's
narrator, identified as a poet-pilgrim on a quest for aesthetic enlightenment, posits as a goal for art a view of the whole that exists outside of
time, the product of an aesthetic quietism that allows the poet to distil
experience to express reality as it exists in memory. As we will see below,
Valle-Inclán's interest in memory and qualitative temporal experience
puts him in conversation with the French philosopher Henri Bergson
and others responding to turn of the century positivism.

Designated by Valle-Inclán as the first volume of his collected works,
The Lamp of Marvels is a product of what Margarita Santos Zas has referred to as the long gestation that characterizes the author's work.[18] As
mentioned, early formulations of central aesthetic principles like a harmony of opposites or a focus on memory as the site of the real appear in
the art critical essays of 1908 and 1912 and in transcripts of conferences
given while touring Argentina with Josefina Blanco in 1910. The treatise
also has important after-effects, notably in *Midnight: Astral Vision of a
Moment of War* but also in Valle-Inclán's works from the 1920s. Without
consideration of the long gestation that characterizes Valle-Inclán's artistic practice and the centrality of *The Lamp of Marvels*, it is easy to
conclude, as many critics have, that there are two opposing periods to
Valle-Inclán's literary production: a conservative period with works set
in rural Galicia or characterized by modernist, escapist tendencies, and
an avant-garde, politically liberal one dating from 1916.[19] Such a characterization ignores biographic details like Valle-Inclán's continuing association with Carlism and, more importantly, constants among the
literary texts; for example, later dramas like *Divinas palabras* (*Divine*

Spanish translations of central texts by Helena Blavatsky as well as editions of
texts from esoteric traditions like the *Guia espiritual* by the heterodox mystic
Miguel de Molinos (1628–1696). Although Valle-Inclán is not known to have been
a member of the Grupo de Estudios Teosóficos Marco Aureliano, the theosophical
group active in Ponte Vedra (Galicia) during the 1910s, he was friends with several
prominent members and his interest in occult practices generally has been well
documented. For a history of theosophy in Spain, see Vílchez Ruiz, 'Las fuentes
y conceptos teosóficos de *La lámpara maravillosa* a la luz de los autógrafos conservados en el legado Valle-Inclán Alsina', *Anales de la literatura española contemporánea*, 41 (2016), pp. 725–50.

18 Santos Zas, 'Introducción a la vida'.

19 This assumed split was perhaps most famously articulated by Pedro Salinas, a
poet who referred to Valle-Inclán as the 'prodigal son' of the more politically en-
gaged 'Generation of '98'. For a discussion of the generational model still prevalent
in Spanish literary studies, see Pereiro Otero, *La escritura modernista*.

Words, 1919) and *Cara de Plata* (*Golden Boy*, 1923), the third work in the *Savage Comedies* trilogy, share characteristics of the so-called first period as examples of rural dramas set in Galicia and yet contain elements of grotesque deformation that point to the *esperpentos*.

Luces de bohemia (*Bohemian Lights*, 1920, 1924) is the first of Valle-Inclán's works to be designated an *esperpento*. In the drama, the text's hero, the blind poet Max Estrella, famously presents a definition of the genre that he 'invents': Spain, according to Max Estrella, is a grotesque deformation of Europe, and, as a result, its tragedy cannot be expressed through classical means but rather must pass through a process of systematic distortion. Illustrating this distortion with a visual metaphor, Max references a group of concave mirrors that lined a local Madrid street (and that were well-known at the time); classical heroes reflected in the distortion produced by these mirrors characterize the *esperpento*. In an intertextual example, when subjected to the distortion of the mirror and, by extension, to the grotesque reality of Madrid in the 1920s, the blind poet Homer transforms into the esperpentic (and arguably noble) figure Max Estrella.

The systematic deformation that the reader/audience encounters in *Bohemian Lights*, and in a series of other theatrical *esperpentos* written in the 1920s, also characterizes Valle-Inclán's prose work from the decade, perhaps most importantly *Tirano Banderas* (*Tyrant Banderas*, 1926), a novel set in Latin America that traces the three days leading to the death of dictator Santos Banderas and that participates in an important narrative genre in Latin American literature, the dictator novel. Set in a non-specific Latin American country and utilizing Spanish idioms from several Latin American countries, *Tyrant Banderas* transforms documentary sources to create a grotesque representation of a non-specific Latin American political reality.

The final years of Valle-Inclán's life were marked by the re-edition of several works and the publication as collections of existing poetry and short stories. In spite of failing health, Valle-Inclán held several political roles in the Second Spanish Republic (1931–36), serving briefly as Conservator of the National Artistic Patrimony (1932) and then as Director of the Academy of Fine Arts in Rome from 1932 until his death in 1936 (although much of his time as Director was spent in Spain).[20]

20 For documentation and a fascinating account of Valle-Inclán's work as Director of the Academy in Rome, see Santos Zas and others, *Todo Valle-Inclán en Roma (1933–1936): edición, anotación, indices, facsimiles* (Universidade de Santiago de Compostela, 2010).

Valle-Inclán died in Santiago de Compostela in January of 1936, months before the Nationalist rebellion that unleashed the Spanish Civil War (1936–39) and ushered in the dictatorship of Francisco Franco. Like those of many of his contemporaries, the works of Valle-Inclán were censored during the Franco period, but in the final years of the dictatorship and after the death of Franco in 1975, the author's work, his theatre in particular, received renewed interest. To take a few examples, *Bohemian Lights* finally premiered in Spain in 1970 in a production directed by José Tamayo, and the *Savage Comedies* were staged in their entirety by José Carlos Plaza for the Centro Dramático Nacional in 1991. More recently, *Divine Words* was staged in New York in 2007 as part of the Lincoln Center Festival, in a production directed by Gerardo Vera of the Centro Dramático Nacional.

Valle-Inclán at the Western Front: The 'Notebook from France'

In 1915, Valle-Inclán was part of a group of authors, artists, and intellectuals to sign a 'Manifiesto de adhesion de las Naciones Aliadas' ('Manifesto of Support for the Allied Nations'), a document that was published in the press in Madrid and then France.[21] Valle-Inclán's role in the manifesto's production, and in particular his relationship with Jacques Chaumie, a French diplomat who had translated some of Valle-Inclán's works and who facilitated the manifesto's publication in France,[22] was in part responsible for his invitation to visit the Western Front as a correspondent for *El Imparcial*.[23] Before leaving for France in May 1916, Valle-Inclán made clear in a published interview that the visit would result not only in the newspaper account but also in a book, the 'concepto' (conception) of which he had already established:

---

21 'La guerra Europea: palabras de algunos españoles', *El Liberal*, 5 July 1915, cited in Bénédicte Vauthier and Margarita Santos Zas, 'Estudio y dossier genético', in Valle-Inclán, *Un día de guerra*, p. 96.

22 Santos Zas presents the history of Valle-Inclán's attempts to have his works translated into French in 'Valle-Inclán en francés: expectativas e realidades', in *Outros verbos, novas lecturas: Valle-Inclán traducido (1906–1936)*, ed. by Rosario Mascato Rey (Consello da Cultura Galega, 2014), pp. 27–38.

23 Vauthier and Santos Zas, 'Estudio y dossier genético', pp. 100–01.

Yo tengo un concepto anterior, yo voy a constatar ese concepto y
no a inventarlo. El arte es siempre una abstracción. [...] La guerra
no se puede ver como unas cuantas granadas que caen aquí o allá,
ni como unos cuantos muertos y heridos que se cuentan luego en
estadísticas: hay que verla desde una Estrella, amigo mío, fuera del
tiempo, fuera del tiempo y del espacio.[24]

(I have a conception in mind; I am going to actualize this conception and not invent it. Art is always an abstraction. [...] One cannot view the war as a few grenades that fall here and there, or as
a few dead and injured people later counted up as statistics; one
needs to see it from a Star, my friend, outside of time, outside of
time and space.)

I will return to Valle-Inclán's comments below but want to stress here
that, from its inception, *Midnight: Astral Vision of a Moment of War*
moves well beyond the eyewitness account one might expect from a
war chronicle, notably positing before experiencing the war the 'astral
vision' which is central to the novel.

While in France, Valle-Inclán travelled to the front on three occa-
sions, each time accompanied by Chaumie and other officials of the
French government. The first visit was to Remiremont in the Vosges
Mountains, from where he took side trips to an observation tower
at Hartmannswillerkopf, and to the towns of Thann, Mittlach, and
Metzeral, among other places; the second was to the Champagne region, where he visited Châlons and, importantly, flew in an aeroplane
for the first time;[25] and the third was back to Champagne to visit the
heavily damaged city of Reims ('Notebook', pp. 110–11; see Fig. 2).

He recorded details from these visits in a diary that contains Valle-
Inclán's impressions of the bombed-out countryside, of his first visit to
the trenches, of generals and the dinners they host, and of anecdotes
that eventually find their way into the texts. The notes also contain

24 Cipriano Rivas Cherif, 'Los españoles y la guerra: el viaje de Valle-Inclán',
España (Madrid), 11 May 1916, cited in Dru Dougherty, *Un Valle-Inclán olvidado:
entrevistas y conferencias* (Fundamentos, 1983), pp. 78–82.
25 Although Valle-Inclán's description of the experience in the notebook is brief,
he elaborates in a letter to Estanislao Pérez Artime (Tanis), 'Yo he volado sobre las
trincheras alemanas, y jamás he sentido una impresión que iguale a ésta en fuerza y
belleza' ('I have flown over the German trenches and have never felt an impression
that matches this in force and beauty'). Cited in Vauthier and Santos Zas, 'Estudio
y dossier genético', p. 128.

FIG. 2. Map indicating location of place names referenced in *Midnight*.

ideas or 'motivos' (motifs) for potential development and, at points, record his reactions to what he experiences. For example, in one section,
he notes a nightmarish distortion produced by the rapid succession of
images he sees from a car window as it moves through the countryside.
The entry is an early formulation of the condensation of time that becomes a defining characteristic of the condensed timespan recorded in
Midnight:

> Acabo de darme la impresión de la pesadilla la acumulación de
> sucesos en un breve espacio de tiempo. El automóvil al desfilar
> por la Carretera dejando atrás montes y valles, la rápida sucesión
> de los paisajes, acumula y junta las emociones como acontece en
> los sueños.[26]

26 Valle-Inclán, *Con el alba*, p. 125. In their introductory study in their edition of
La media noche, Vauthier and Santos Zas explore the condensed timespan of the
text (p. 127).

(The accumulation of events in a brief duration of time just gave me the impression of a nightmare. The automobile filing down the Highway, leaving behind mountains and valleys, the quick succession of these landscapes, accumulate and join emotions together as they occur in dreams.)

What Valle-Inclán witnesses, the record of what he experiences, becomes source material for the two-part newspaper chronicle *Un día de guerra (visión estelar)* ('A Day at War (Astral Vision)'), and then for the novel *Midnight: Astral Vision of a Moment of War.*[27] The notebook contains references to experiences that are contained in both. For example, in the notebook, Valle-Inclán writes, 'escucho el relato de los muertos a la vela' ('I hear the story of the dead at sail', 'Notebook', p. 153), in what appears to be a reference to a memorable anecdote that is retold in both the newspaper chronicle and in *Midnight*. The bodies of German soldiers wash onto the shore in Vuerne on the western coast of Belgium; they are discovered by marines who ask their lieutenant if they can attach sails to the bodies, transforming them into a fleet of feluccas, a type of traditional wooden fishing boat, to bury them at sea. The anecdote ends with a young sailor exclaiming in Breton, '¡Madre del Señor! ¡Ya no tengo miedo a los muertos!' ('Mother of God! I am no longer afraid of the Dead!', *Midnight*, p. 51), a line transcribed in the notebook as part of another anecdote involving a Breton soldier ('Notebook', p. 153).[28] Clearly, in both the newspaper chronicle and in *Midnight* Valle-Inclán moves well beyond an eyewitness account, here including a story that occurred in a place to which he had not travelled.

Although there are changes to the placement of this episode and to individual words, the versions contained in the chronicle and in *Midnight* are similar. This is not always the case, however, and the omissions and additions between the two texts serve as important keys to the different foci, what Valle-Inclán referred to as their conceptions. In an illustrative

27 The two parts of the newspaper chronicle are subtitled 'Parte primera: La Media Noche' ('Part I: Midnight') and 'Segunda parte: En la luz del día' ('Part II: In the Light of the Day'). There are nine instalments with thirty-four fragments in Part I, published between October and December 1916, and four instalments with seven fragments in Part II, published in January and February of 1917. See Dougherty, 'Valle-Inclán, corresponsal de guerra', for a discussion of contemporary World War I chronicles published by Spanish correspondents.

28 The episode appears in chapters 13 to 15 of Valle-Inclán, *Un día de guerra* as sections of the instalments of 11 and 14 October 1916. It comprises chapters 10 to 12 of *Midnight* in the present translation.

example, Valle-Inclán's treatment of aviation, which he clearly finds of great interest, varies greatly in the serialized chronicle and in *Midnight*. As mentioned above, the notebook contains a brief reference to the author's first flight, which is contained within a description of an airfield and aviators:

> Belleza de los aviones. Campo de aviación. Llanura verde, con flores amarillas. Hangares pintadas de verde en las techumbres, para no ser fácilmente distinguidos. Vuelo en un avión. Aspecto del paisaje. El viento. Combate de aviones. Los aviadores — jóvenes y alegres — La visita de las cocottes. El aviador por brutalidad, por entereza, por misticismo, por amor a la ciencia nueva, por gallardía, por aristocracia y atavismo de aventuras y glorias militares. ('Notebook', p. 162)

> (The beauty of aeroplanes. Aviation field. Green plain with yellow flowers. Hangers with roofs painted green so they will not be easily discovered. Flight in an aeroplane. Appearance of the landscape. The wind. Aeroplane battles. The pilots — young and happy — The visit of the coquettes. A pilot, through brutality, through fortitude, through love of new science, through courage, through aristocracy and adventurous atavism and military glories.)

These notes are preceded by a long description of a visit to the trenches near Châlons, which is disrupted by fighter planes: 'El aire se abre con un aullido de gata parida cuando la bala lo rasga' ('The air opens up with a howl like a cat giving birth when the bullet rips through', 'Notebook', p. 161).[29] A French plane is hit and Valle-Inclán, the members of his entourage, and the soldiers who escort them discover the bodies of two pilots which have been so badly mutilated that they need to be buried on the spot. A clearly shaken Valle-Inclán records these injuries in graphic detail in the notebook.

Many details from these notes are expanded upon and included both in the serialized chronicle and in *Midnight*.[30] For example, both accounts include a description of the airfield and hangar. Part I of the newspaper chronicle, however, embeds this description in a scene that

---

29 This striking simile appears in *Midnight* as part of Chapter 9, where it is recontextualized to refer to the sound of cannon fire.

30 The episode appears in chapters 5 to 8 of Part I of *Un día de guerra*, in the instalment published on 23 October 1916. The episode takes place in Chapter 6 of *Midnight*.

develops over four short chapters. In the sequence, a group of pilots prepares for a night mission and is visited by the coquettes whom Valle-Inclán references briefly in the notebook: we read the pilots' banter with the women and dialogue that provides the airmen's different reactions to an upcoming mission. The death of the French pilots is separate from this scene, appearing not in Part I but in the final instalment to Part II, and thus closing the serialized newspaper account. Like the scene with the coquettes, the later scene includes dialogue, here recording the soldiers' initial hopes that it is a German plane that has been shot down and their resignation at the discovery of the French pilots' bodies. A graphic description of the bodies, which reproduces that found in the notebook, serves as the sombre final sentences to the newspaper chronicle:

> Una masa sangrienta: Los cascos entrados hasta los hombros, las piernas rotas, el pecho hundido, las ropas chamuscadas. Al poner [los cuerpos] en una angarilla sus despojos de desbordan fueran y caen en una masa roja y líquida. Se les cava allí la sepultura. Un capellán que tiene la medalla de guerra, reza el responso. Los soldados descubiertos, permanecen silenciosos. El avión sigue ardiendo. Por el camino avanza un soldado con dos cruces.[31]

> (A bloody mass: Helmets pushed down into shoulders, broken legs, a sunken chest, scorched clothing. When placing them [the bodies] in wheelbarrows, the remains spill out and fall in a red, liquid mass. They dig the graves there. A chaplain wearing a war medal prays for the dead. The soldiers, helmets removed, are silent. The plane continues to burn. A soldier with two crosses comes down the road.)

Given the length of these two sequences in the serialized chronicle, the dialogue that distinguishes one pilot from another in the hanger scene, and the graphic description of the pilots' bodies that provides a dramatic, disturbing end to the account, their absence from *Midnight* is surprising.

As mentioned above, *Midnight* also includes a description of the airfield, but instead of dialogue among pilots that distinguishes them one from the other, the narrator focusses on aeroplanes and the destruction they bring: 'Over the two hundred leagues of muddy trenches, rockets open their roses, searchlights tremble, and in the shadows, aeroplanes carry their cargo of explosives to destroy, to burn, to kill...' (p.

31 Valle-Inclán, *Un día de guerra*, p. 95. The account appears in 'Notebook', p. 162.

44, ellipses in the original). In the sentence that follows, the narrator zooms in to describe the occupants of these planes: 'Cheerful pilots occupy the cockpits, crazed with air-born vertigo, like heroes from old tragedies crazed with erotic vertigo. Dressed in furs, with large, round glasses and round, leather helmets, they have an embryonic form and darkly evoke scientific monsters' (p. 44). Although the scene ends with a mention of pilots downed during the night's battle, their mutilated bodies are not described but rather the focus moves to the work of soldiers who bring the planes into the camouflaged hanger. The pilots as described in both texts are audacious and brave; in *Midnight*, however, they are not given characteristics that would identify them as individuals but rather are presented as types. The admiration the narrator expresses for their bravery links them to mythic heroes and, at the same time, is tempered by the more sinister reference to the technology that allows for their destructive potential. In an example of a harmony of opposites, a concept which, as we will see below, is central to Valle-Inclán's aesthetics as developed in *The Lamp of Marvels*, the pilots evoke both heroes and monsters.

In their introductory study of *Midnight: Astral Vision of a Moment of War*, Vauthier and Santos Zas argue convincingly that although there is some material shared between the serialized chronicle and the novel, Valle-Inclán conceived of the two as different projects.[32] There are formal changes between them: some sequences, like the scene with the coquettes discussed above, do not appear in *Midnight*, and no material from the second part of the serialized chronicle appears there. As a result, a primary mode of presentation shifts from the dialogue of the newspaper account, which identifies and differentiates characters, to the narrative of *Midnight*, which is focalized through the narrator's perspective, through his view from the stars. Although some individual characters are identified in *Midnight*, no one receives undue focus but rather functions as part of a mosaic created by the whole. Further, as Vauthier and Santos Zas comment, in eliminating Part II of the serialized text, the time span is reduced even further from 'a day' to the twelve-hour span of *Midnight*. This reduced temporal span, together with spatial distancing, allow for an accumulation of perspectives and voices that appear to be simultaneous.

In addition to cutting material, Valle-Inclán includes new material in

32 Part II, 'In the Light of Day', was discovered by Roberta Salper in 1968. Although Valle-Inclán did not include this material in *Midnight*, it was included in subsequent editions of the text, creating what Vauthier and Santos Zas argue is a 'contaminated edition'; see 'Estudio y dossier genético', p. 27.

Midnight and modifies existing chapters, introducing additional chapter breaks and rearranging their order. Perhaps most significantly, he also adds the introductory 'Brief Notice', which lays out the aesthetic conception underlying an astral view of the war. As we will see, the formal changes between the two texts, together with the 'Brief Notice', move it from the account of a (fictionalized) witness that we find in the serialized chronicle to that of the poet 'who deserves to be called Seer' (p. 40) who is introduced in the 'Brief Notice' and whose perspective views the action from above and distils the individual experience of independent witnesses into a collective whole.[33]

A focus on the limited perspective of the witness is a central concern of *Midnight*'s 'Brief Notice'. As we saw in the interview he gave before leaving for the Western Front cited above, Valle-Inclán discussed his plans for an eventual book based on his experiences, the conception of which had already been determined. Remarking in the interview that an individual perspective necessarily creates a fragmented view of the war, the view of 'a few grenades that fall here and there' or of 'a few dead and injured people later counted up as statistics', Valle-Inclán expresses the need to overcome the limited perspective of the witness. This is, of course, the situation of Valle-Inclán, whose initials close *Midnight*'s 'Brief Notice', and who is himself a witness with a limited perspective of the war.[34]

The narrator of the 'Brief Notice' observes that an account of war depends very much on individual experience and, thus, is random, 'born of the human and geometric limitations that prohibit us from being in more than one place at the same time':

> And like anyone who must take many days to traverse the enormous battle-front stretching from the Alsatian Mountains down to the seacoast, the narrator adjusts the war and its unforeseen events to the measure of his own stride: Battles begin when his eyes begin to see them: The terrible sound of the war stops when he moves away from its tragic settings and returns when he comes closer. All stories are limited by the geometry of the narrator's position. (p. 39)

33 The astral vision that defines the narrator's perspective refers to the goal of dwelling in a centre of astral light. The identification of the narrator as 'Seer' makes explicit the esoteric register of the 'Brief Notice', which culminates in a reference to the twelfth-century alchemist Artephius. See n. 3 to the translation for further details about this figure.

34 Vauthier and Santos Zas, 'Estudio y dossier genético', p. 111.

Valle-Inclán exploits the expressive potential of nonstandard punctuation throughout the novel. Here, the series of colons with a capital letter
following suggests that the forward movement of a witness is impeded
by one of the war's 'unforeseen events'. The colons serve as a visual cue
to the problem of the witness's limited perspective, suggesting the type
of fragmented vision referred to by the narrator. The goal for the short
novel is to move from this partial perspective to one that distils individual stories into a collective whole, 'the vision of all people who were
in the war and saw at the same time all its settings, all its occurrences'
(p. 40).

In the 'Brief Notice', the partial perspective of the witness is described
graphically through a description of soldiers returning home in which
the soldiers' fragmented bodies metonymically express a horrific yet
individual experience:

> When the soldiers from France return to their villages, and the
> blind wander down paths with their guides, and those who don't
> have legs beg at the doors of churches, and one-armed amputees
> run from place to place in the happy role of go-betweens; when at
> the family hearth the dead are named and prayed for, each mouth
> will have a different story and the stories will number hundreds
> of thousands, an expression of many other visions that in the end
> will be distilled into one vision, a sign of all things. (pp. 39–40)

Importantly, the narrator joins together the stories indexed by the fragmented bodies to create a view of the whole, of 'one vision, a sign of
all'. He posits that such a perspective would allow for a more complete
representation of the war, of 'a vision, an emotion, and a conception
of [it]' distinct in every sense from that of 'the wretched witness who
is subjected to the geometric laws of corporeal and mortal matter' (p.
39). If the text's conception is a view of the whole created by the Seer's
distant perspective and synthetic powers, here it is enabled by an 'emotion', an 'intuition [...] outside of space and time' (p. 39). As we will see,
both principles — the view of the whole that serves as the conception
of *Midnight* and the force of emotion that enables this view — are central to the narrator's quest in the aesthetic treatise *The Lamp of Marvels*.

Published only a few months before Valle-Inclán travelled to the
Western Front, *The Lamp of Marvels* lays out the theory for what the
author attempts in practice in *Midnight*, a relationship that is made
explicit in the final lines of the 'Brief Notice' through a reference to a
lamp that allows for aesthetic enlightenment. Citing the twelfth-century

alchemist Artephius, the narrator explains in a section that is set off from the text by italics:

> *I lit the lamp at the edge of midnight. I placed myself in front of it, and my shadow covered the wall. I opened the book and spelled the words that disembody a soul wanting to look at the world outside of geometry.* (p. 41)

The techniques Valle-Inclán employs in *Midnight* are the product of a narrator who attempts to write with 'astral vision', here expressed as that of a world 'outside of geometry'. Announcing a conception for the eventual novel before leaving for the Western Front, Valle-Inclán makes clear in the final lines of the 'Brief Notice' that the theoretical grounding for this conception has been laid out in *The Lamp of Marvels*.[35]

A Theory behind Astral Vision: 'The Lamp of Marvels'

Like the narrator of *Midnight*, the narrator in *The Lamp of Marvels* refers to the limited perspective of a witness. Employing language not of war but of an esoteric journey, this aesthetic treatise traces the path of its pilgrim-poet narrator to aesthetic quietism, which, as we will see, is analogous to the emotion that enables the 'astral vision' referred to above and that allows for artistic creation. Despite the very different contexts, the pilgrim-poet of *The Lamp of Marvels* and the poet 'who deserves to be called Seer' of *Midnight* share a desire to transcend the limits of an individual perspective bound by time and space.

In the introductory section of *The Lamp of Marvels*, the narrator makes a distinction between meditation, the paths of which are 'always chronological and of the very substance of the hours', and contemplation, 'an absolute mode of knowledge, an amiable, delectable, and kind intuition through which the soul enjoys the beauty of the world without discourse and in the divine tenebra' (p. 3). If meditation, according to the narrator, is a type of reason bound by discourse that allows for

---

35 Virginia Garlitz lays out this connection between theory and practice in 'La estética de Valle-Inclán en "La media noche" y "En la luz del día"', *Revista de estudios hispánicos*, 16 (1989), pp. 21–30. See also Arcadio López-Casanova, 'Valle-Inclán en Francia: "Un día de guerra"', *Valle Inclán (1898–1998): escenarios: seminario internacional Universidade de Santiago de Compostela, noviembre–diciembre, 1998*, ed. by Margarita Santos Zas (Universidade de Santiago de Compostela, 2000), pp. 159–78.

a partial truth, contemplation leads to 'the same deduced truth once it becomes part of our being, forgotten the method through which reason is intertwined with reason, thought with thought'. While meditation allows one to 'love each creature separately and in itself', contemplation allows one to transcend meditative paths to reach the summit that affords a view of a whole. Contemplation is 'the supreme comprehension of the world' not accessible to 'meditating reason' (p. 4). In this brief introduction to *The Lamp of Marvels*, the question of how to leave behind an individual, partial perspective — the problem raised explicitly in *Midnight*'s 'Brief Notice' — is also raised, albeit in an esoteric register. Through the successive stages presented in *The Lamp of Marvels*, the poet-pilgrim leaves behind meditative paths, which are not without value but are fragmented by space and time, for experience facilitated through contemplation.

The Lamp of Marvels posits that it is a view from above that allows for an experience of the whole, or, in a central image from the text, that allows the pilgrim-poet to create a circle of his experiences, centring himself within 'luz astral' ('astral light').[36] As several critics have noted, this practice of making oneself a centre is presented in various formulations throughout the treatise.[37] It is the goal of a 'harmonía de contrarios' ('harmony of opposites'), a practice in which contradictory concepts and perspectives are put into conversation, effecting not synthesis but rather a balance in which the centre recognizes the force of each. It is also the goal of a view from above in which the subject can witness a whole not afforded by a more immediate perspective.[38] Both concepts — a harmony of opposites and a view from above — are operative in *Midnight*.

In an early chapter of *The Lamp of Marvels*, the narrator recounts a journey through the mountains. He remarks that after smoking a hash pipe,[39] he ascends paths that overlook the land surrounding his childhood home, paths he claims explicitly never before to have travelled:

> We were traversing the lands of Salnés [...] on which I had grown from tender lad to dark-haired youth. Yet I had never set foot on

36 Garlitz, 'El ocultismo finisecular'.
37 Garlitz notes the importance of the concept to Valle-Inclán's aesthetics in choosing it as the title of her foundational study, *El centro del círculo*.
38 Carmen Vílchez Ruiz discusses Valle-Inclán's development of the term in precursor texts in 'De las ideas estéticas'.
39 Interestingly, this detail is also found in the conclusion of *Midnight*'s 'Brief Notice', announcing the author's desire to access aesthetic quietude.

that mountainous terrain. We rode so high above them that the valleys appeared distant, miniaturized, intensified with the translucence of lacquer. (p. 15)

As he contemplates the landscape from above, he is surprised to recognize details: 'I knew the crossroads in the middle of the fields, the shallow places of the brooks, the shadows of the enclosures' (p. 15). Unable to physically see these details from the summit, he realizes that his vision synthesizes childhood memories of these spaces into a 'cifra', a sign of the whole. The narrator understands this synthesis of valley spaces to be a vision in which his soul is 'untethered', and he experiences the 'ecstasy of that wholeness':

> With coordinated and profound joy, I felt as one with the shadow of the tree, the flight of the bird, the Summit of the mountain. The land of Salnés was wholly in my ken by the grace of that joyous and theological vision. I remained captive, my eyes sealed by the imprint of that valley — deep, quiet, green, with drizzle and sunlight — which in cyclical comprehensiveness summed up all my chronological knowledge of the land of Salnés. (p. 16)

From the mountain's heights, the narrator's childhood memories of individual spaces, seen here not as paths offering a fragmentary view but from above, are brought to the present to form a vision of an atemporal whole. Like the shadow created by a tree, the memories are undifferentiated and temporally condensed, and viewed not as discrete but, in a reference to the goals of contemplation seen above, in their 'cyclical comprehensiveness'.

The effect of a distanced perspective, of course, is one shared by the narrator of *Midnight*, in which astral vision is called on to allow for a view of the whole and for the distillation of experiences and voices into a collective. At the same time that the narrator of *The Lamp of Marvels* obtains a comprehensive view of the valley, he brings past experiences to the temporal present, condensing the temporal sphere in an effect that 'aspires to be eternal' (p. 16). In *Midnight*, the narrator's view of the two hundred leagues that make up the Western Front comprises what the narrator 'sees' as he brings the multiple spaces, collective and singular actors, and diverse events to the temporal present in a condensation of the temporal sphere. Like the accumulation of images within a condensed temporal frame that Valle-Inclán experiences as he travels by car to the front and records in his notebook, these multiple images are viewed as within an undifferentiated whole. Although in the anecdote from *The Lamp of Marvels* the distillation of experience concerns memories from the childhood of the narrator — from one perspective over time — its effect is similar in *Midnight* where the experiences of individual soldiers, whose maimed bodies serve as emblem of their particular and thus partial experience, are brought to the narrator's temporal present.

The chapter of *The Lamp of Marvels* concludes, as does each chapter of the treatise, with a gloss that serves as summary of the concept illustrated. While the gloss reiterates the central action of dwelling in a circle formed by one's experiences, here the memories evoked are tied to emotions: 'Ecstasy is the joy of being captive in the circle of an emotion so pure that it aspires to be eternal' (p. 16). Valle-Inclán's view from above allows him to make a 'circle' of his experience by bringing memories to the present; importantly, this circle is enabled by an 'eternal emotion', by the quietude that allows for a different temporal experience. Like the 'Brief Notice' of *Midnight*, in which the narrator posits a refinement of emotion and an intuition outside of time and space that distils the experience of soldiers who went to the front, here the emotion resulting from the mountain view allows for a vision that transcends discrete spaces and moments in time. In both texts a contemplative state produces quietude, allowing the subject to transcend spatial and temporal limits to experience a view of the whole.

In *The Lamp of Marvels* and *Midnight: Astral Vision of a Moment of War*, Valle-Inclán explores the problem of a viewer (whether poet, pilgrim, soldier, or witness) whose perspective is limited by what he sees and whose language further fragments this experience. Attempts to transcend barriers of time and space implicate language which, as a rational system that develops chronologically, fragments experience and introduces perspective. The project of both texts, and of interest to Valle-Inclán across his writing, is an attempt to transcend these and other barriers to create outside of a limited perspective, to transcend the limitations of what Henri Bergson has termed quantitative expressions of time, of which language is one.

Henri Bergson's theories of time, memory, and perception have proven helpful as a means to identify and explore the theory expressed through the dense esoteric citation that characterizes *The Lamp of Marvels*.[40] In particular, Bergson's distinction between quantitative and

---

40 Although it is doubtful that the two ever met, Valle-Inclán's library included four of Bergson's works. Bergson's philosophy was of great interest in intellectual circles in which Valle-Inclán played a fundamental role during the first decades

qualitative temporal conceptions maps onto Valle-Inclán's understanding of meditation, with its limits as a rational system, and contemplation, 'an absolute mode of knowledge'. Bergson opposes positivism and other attempts to quantify human experience with an inner experience of time in which events are radically heterogeneous and interpenetrate, one within the other. This temporal continuity, what he terms *durée* (duration), is a subjective experience of consciousness prior to its expression as chronology or in language, both of which are rational systems that spatialize experience.[41] Like Valle-Inclán, who claims that contemplation is 'a quiet intuition [...] through which the soul enjoys the beauty of the world without discourse' (*Lamp of Marvels*, p. 4), Bergson's duration is prior to language and fundamentally altered by it. In this sense, astral vision both is a figure for Valle-Inclán's understanding of contemplation as developed in *The Lamp of Marvels* and has parallels with Bergson's duration as an attempt to access experience outside of a fragmented perspective.

of the century, and authors who were contemporaries of Valle-Inclán described aspects of Valle-Inclán's works in terms of Bergson. Mascato Rey lists the following Spanish translations of Bergson and their dates of publication: *Materia y memoria: ensayo sobre la relación del cuerpo con el espíritu* (1900); *La evolución creadora* (1912); *La risa: ensayo sobre la significación de lo cómico* (1914); *Ensayo sobre los datos inmediatos de la conciencia* (1925): Rosario Mascato Rey, 'Tras la huella de Bergson: fundamentos para un estudio del intuicionismo en Valle-Inclán', *Anales de la literatura española contemporánea*, 34.3 (2009), pp. 67–94. Several scholars have mentioned connections between the two authors. See, for example, Rodolfo Cardona, 'El tiempo de la *Sonata de otoño*', in *Ramón de Valle-Inclán: An Appraisal of His Life and Works*, ed. by Anthony N. Zahareas (Las Américas, 1986), pp. 216–23; Ciriaco Morrón Arroyo, '*La lámpara maravillosa* y la ecuación estética', in *Ramón de Valle-Inclán*, ed. by Zahareas, pp. 443–59; Vauthier and Santos Zas, 'Estudio y dossier genético'. Outside of the work of Emiliano Bellini ('El recuerdo almacenado: estética del recuerdo en Valle-Inclán y Proust', *Rivista di Filologia e Letterature Ispaniche*, 6 (2003), pp. 349–56), Drumm ('Henri Bergson on Time, Perception and Memory and Ramón del Valle-Inclán's *La lámpara maravillosa*', *Anales de la literatura española contemporánea*, 40 (2015), pp. 19–42), and Mascato Rey ('Tras la huella de Bergson'), however, there have been no full-scale studies. For a discussion of Bergson's influence on other Spanish authors, see Benjamin Fraser, *Encounters with Bergson(ism) in Spain: Reconciling Philosophy, Literature, Film and Urban Space* (University of North Carolina Department of Romance Languages, 2010).

41 Suzanne Guerlac, 'Thinking in Time: Henri Bergson (an Interdisciplinary Conference)', *MLN*, 120.5 (2005), pp. 1091–98 (p. 1095). For an excellent introduction to Bergson's philosophy see Suzanne Guerlac, *Thinking in Time: An Introduction to Henri Bergson* (Cornell University Press, 2006).

Bergson understands aesthetic and spiritual experience to be a means to break through the automatic response that allows for action, the immediate goal and limit of quantitative systems of thought. If language necessarily fragments qualitative experience, reducing it to a rational system that allows for action in the world (like cause and effect, for example), aesthetic experience breaks free from this type of response to one's immediate needs, enabling an observer to access life as experienced within an undifferentiated whole. In a much-cited example, Bergson likens duration to listening to a melody in which we perceive individual notes within a musical phrase. The analogy serves two functions: first, it exemplifies how an aesthetic experience like listening to melody breaks one free from the automatic response that characterizes quantitative time; the contemplation of art allows humans to experience the flow of life outside of an immediate need for action. Second, because the notes within a musical phrase are both singular and integrated within the melody, the analogy points to the impossibility of representing duration. Just as it is not possible to alter one note without affecting the musical phrase as a whole, our qualitative experience is both singular (made up of discrete experiences) and undifferentiated within the whole that comprises our subjective experiences of life; to represent one aspect is to alter the effect of the other.

This second point illustrates a problem that Bergson shares with Valle-Inclán: the impossibility of fully expressing either duration or contemplation. Because duration cannot be expressed through rational systems like language, which necessarily fragment it, Bergson turns to a series of analogies — like the example of melody above — which illustrate aspects of the concept without attempting to fully define it. Astral vision is Valle-Inclán's solution, becoming one of a series of practices that Valle-Inclán employs to mitigate the fragmentation produced by language. Vauthier and Santos Zas conclude that, like other techniques Valle-Inclán explores throughout his literary career (for example, attempting to transcend time and space through occult practices, smoking hashish, or expressing the view from an aeroplane in flight), astral vision is an attempt to 'alcanzar la intuición quietista' ('achieve the quietist intuition') that is posited in *The Lamp of Marvels*.[42]

Both duration and astral vision align with central theories of literary modernism which attempt to represent simultaneity, from Cubist perspectivism to stream of consciousness. Valle-Inclán's astral vision, with its expansive spatial field and condensed temporal one, and whose

42 Vauthier and Santos Zas, 'Estudio y dossier genético', p. 144.

action presumably occurs simultaneously to its writing, makes its own substantial contribution to central problems of the period.[43]

Valle-Inclán's Disclaimer: 'I Have Failed in my Resolve'

In the penultimate paragraph of the 'Brief Notice', Valle-Inclán characterizes *Midnight* a failure:

> I, clumsy and vain, wanted to be at the centre and to have an astral vision of the war, outside of geometry and chronology, as if my soul, already disembodied, were looking at the earth from a star. I have failed in my resolve. (p. 40)

This surprising disclaimer undercuts the premise of astral vision at the point it has been intriguingly articulated. Although it may simply be an ironic comment that points to the audacity of Valle-Inclán's claims, or a recognition of the impossibility that writing can ever represent the fullness of an atemporal synthesis of multiple voices viewed simultaneously, the disclaimer also points to several tensions in the novel.[44]

Among these tensions is the unacknowledged bias of Valle-Inclán's narrator: if the view from the stars allows for collective vision, the narrator's perspective in *Midnight: Astral Vision of a Moment of War* is remarkably partial, making clear from the first chapter its allegiance to Allied forces, those of the French in particular. Further, although the narrator makes claims about the harmony and 'ideal architecture' (p. 67) of war when viewed from the stars, this abstraction is met

43 Vauthier and Santos Zas cite Roger Shattuck for context concerning modernist artists' interest in expressions of simultaneity. In Shattuck's view, simultaneity in the arts 'aprehende lo que, para nuestra cultura, es un tipo nuevo de coherencia, una nueva unidad de la experiencia' ('apprehend what is in our culture a new type of coherence, a new unity of experience'; Roger Shattuck, *La época de los banquetes*, pp. 284–85, cited in Vauthier and Santos Zas, 'Estudio y dossier genético', pp. 143–44). See also Amparo de Juan Bolufer, *La técnica narrativa en Valle-Inclán* (Universidade de Santiago de Compostela, 2000), pp. 257–58.

44 Among the possible explanations is Valle-Inclán's reference in the 'Brief Notice' to an inability to synthesize fully the experience of 'a day at war' (p. 40, in capital letters in the original). In this sense the 'failure' Valle-Inclán refers to concerns the reduced twelve-hour timespan of *Midnight*, which is a reduction of the full twenty-four-hour account of the newspaper chronical, also titled *A Day at War*. For a discussion of this point, see Vauthier and Santos Zas, 'Estudio y dossier genético', p. 142.

by the representation of particular, horrific scenes of devastation. In *Midnight*, the problem of the witness's partial perspective has not been fully resolved. As Dru Dougherty concludes, the text is the product of a 'narrador doblado' ('doubled narrator'), of both the witness and Seer referred to in the 'Brief Notice', and reflects two modes of representing the war: 'una mítica y heróica, la otra empírica y documental' ('one mythic and heroic, the other empirical and documentary').[45] Arguing that this doubled perspective puts in question the idea of modern war as heroic, Dougherty concludes that the unresolved tension in the text expresses the anguish of many soldiers who discover that old ways of justifying war are empty of meaning.[46]

We see an example of the tension between witness and Seer, between a documentary and mythologizing perspective, in the movement from newspaper chronicle to *Midnight*. As discussed above, the newspaper chronicle ends horrifically with a graphic image of the bodies of two pilots that have been so severely damaged they cannot be moved. The pilots are buried at the site of their death. This scene, the product of a documentary perspective, is removed in *Midnight* and, in general, the narrator's view in the novel anonymizes violence, or at least a graphic description of the physical destruction inflicted on bodies, a process which at several points in the novel leads to an uncomfortable myth-ification of war. Human bodies become objects, for example, in the scene in which Allied soldiers rig sails to the bodies of German soldiers who have washed ashore, turning them into boats. Notably, the soldiers' fear of death diminishes through this process: a young soldier exclaims, 'Mother of God! I am no longer afraid of the dead!' (p. 51).

Even in those scenes that describe the violence of battle, the narrator's gaze moves quickly to document the destruction instead of its after-effects on individuals. For example, one chapter notes the rapidity of machine gun fire that results in 'diverse modes of dying': 'Some [soldiers] fall like effigies, grotesquely folding their legs; others open their arms and are flattened against the ground; others bend slowly onto the shoulder of a comrade' (p. 49). I will return below to the mechanization of violence illustrated in this scene but for now want to point out that the focus of the description is not violence experienced as an individual

---

45 Dougherty, 'Valle-Inclán, corresponsal de guerra'.
46 Dougherty, 'Valle-Inclán, corresponsal de guerra', p. 571. Dougherty later cites John Lyon, who claims that Valle-Inclán moves from a glorification of war in early texts like the *Carlist War* trilogy to question 'the sordid and essentially unheroic realities of life at the front in a war of commercial interests' (p. 578, n. 24).

tragedy but rather its overall effect, a technique that creates a type of depersonalized detachment or even aestheticization. When two French soldiers volunteer to fix a broken communication wire, their bravery is met with a death whose description transcends physical violence: 'A grenade explodes, and one [soldier] falls on the other: They twist tenderly towards each other, without horror, like two brothers who kiss' (p. 46). One effect of the perspective supplied by astral vision in Midnight is to anonymize death through the distancing of bodies or the valorization of individual actions as heroic through their aestheticization.

Unlike the graphic representation of the pilots' mutilated bodies in the final instalment of the newspaper chronicle, the final chapter of *Midnight* does not document the destruction of individual bodies but rather presents a panoramic view of the front at dawn. The narrator's gaze moves across the field of vision to enumerate the soldiers' actions: they return from the battlefield, slaughter animals to provide food for the camp, bury the dead. In images that return to those of the first chapters, the gaze pulls back to describe convoys of munitions as they move towards the site of the next battle, passing though destroyed villages and farms. The final image of the novel is distanced even further to focus on the desolate landscape, 'uninterrupted from the north coast to the Alsatian Mountains' (p. 73). The landscape is personified in the final line to focus on the mutilation not of bodies but of the land. The narrator concludes, 'In the light of the new day, the land, mutilated by war, has a pained expression, intense and terrible' (p. 73).

This movement away from violence inflicted on human bodies to focus on a personified landscape and war as an abstraction, one effect of the distanced perspective that characterizes astral vision, is announced in *Midnight* in a chapter which explicitly mythologizes war. The narrator summarizes: 'What magnificent fury! What crashing and rebounding, what mythic strength demonstrated by the assault in the trenches!' Acknowledging that the heroic perspective of the battle afforded by astral vision fades when viewed up close in 'the tumult of body on body', the narrator insists that these individual actions 'find a harmonious link' that 'only the eyes of the initiated can grasp' (p. 67). Tying this harmony to the generative power of war, the narrator claims:

> The soul of a people is eternal because of war. Generative desire is rekindled by it like a torch in a wind that strives to put it out. Only the threat of death perpetuates earthly forms, only death makes the world divine. (p. 67)

Here the tremendous loss of war and destruction of individual human bodies is given significance as a divine battle that gives meaning to life.

Interestingly, in spite of these and other attempts to dissociate the effects of violence on humans from what is posited as its mythic significance, the distanced bodies keep coming back: wounded soldiers beg for help, or, in an extended sequence, the narrator recounts the trauma of two sisters impregnated by German soldiers. In another scene, soldiers discover a dog swimming in a flooded trench, 'holding the arm of a sinking body in his teeth. [The soldiers] see a pale hand. The dog swims towards the light' (p. 63). Reminiscent of the description of maimed soldiers that we find in the 'Brief Notice', this metonymic representation insists that human beings — whose fragmented bodies display the violence of war — not be erased, making explicit the reality that dead and injured bodies are never far from the surface. The perspective of a witness confronting the devastating effects of war on individual victims interrupts a more distant, often heroic, view from the stars to create the tension noted by Dougherty.

In both modes — as witness and as Seer — the narrator celebrates Allied forces, the French in particular, rejecting the impartiality implied by one who claims a synthesis of the 'hundreds of thousands' of stories allowed for by astral vision (p. 40). From the very first chapters of *Midnight*, the narrator extolls the virtues of the 'Latin wolf', comparing this force to the negative 'barbarian German, bastard of all tradition' (p. 43). Although there are some examples of negative behaviour on the part of the Allies, in general they are presented as united and heroic.[47] To give a few examples, at the end of a scene focusing on wounded soldiers, the narrator concludes, anticipating later claims of the generative potential of war, that 'the pain of the war shakes and restores the soul of France!' (p. 49); the unity of a group of French artillerymen whose 'souls are joined in brotherhood' is described as a result of the 'religion of war' (p. 59); and when describing the French soldiers' disdain for their adversaries, the narrator remarks:

> For the French soldiers, feelings of human dignity are rooted in a hatred of hierarchies: The Marseillaise moves them to tears, and

---

47 Examples of the characterization of actions by the Allied forces that are less than heroic include the admission by a French lieutenant as he witnesses the electrocution of two French scouts that the Germans have imitated French actions in Indochina (Chapter 6), and the refusal of British forces to take prisoners in chapters 37 and 38, an action which contrasts with the clemency of the French.

from old revolutions they have the sentimental idea of an almost forgotten melodrama in which princes and kings are always trai-tors. (p. 62)

German soldiers, on the other hand, receive negative characterization: the doctor caring for the sisters impregnated by German soldiers gen-eralizes from this action to conclude that the Germans demonstrate 'a hatred of the classical world' (p. 56); when it becomes clear that German forces will lose a battle, the soldiers turn on their commanders, 'indif-ferent to victory, indifferent to hope' (p. 59); German commanders use alcohol to motivate their troops and tie soldiers to their machine guns so they cannot desert (p. 59); and when the soldiers are confronted with imprisonment, they beg their captors like 'dispirited oxen' (p. 69).

That the narrator celebrates Allied actions and unity both from the perspective of the witness and of the Seer complicates the tension that Dougherty identifies. Because the documentary perspective of the wit-ness is not neutral but rather celebrates the heroism of French soldiers and citizens confronted by particular horrors and terrible loss, heroic action is put in conversation with mythic claims about war's regen-erative potential. In this sense, and in spite of the destruction that is unleashed by new technologies in World War I, the Allied forces are motivated by a heroism that continues that of a mythologized past.

Astral Vision and Ethical Action

In her work on Henri Bergson's reception during World War I, Donna V. Jones explores how Bergson's duration, what she terms his 'intui-tive perceptions of experience' and 'worldly mysticism', was co-opted by German intellectuals to argue for the positive effects of war.[48] War broke down 'fragmented bourgeois reality to create a mystical expe-rience of dynamic, inclusive oneness'. Opposing 'instrumental intelli-gence and the classificatory logic of positivism' with an experience of being part of a collective in which 'no single member's destiny is differ-ent from any other's', Bergson's theories were understood to allow for community and a regeneration of the German people.[49]

48 Donna V. Jones, 'Mysticism and War: Reflections on Bergson and His Recep-tion during World War I', *Journal of French and Francophone Philosophy*, 24.2 (2016), pp. 10–20.
49 Jones, 'Mysticism and War', p. 16. Jones returns to the example of one note

The misappropriation of Bergson's theories by Georg Simmel, Max Scheler, and other German intellectuals caused Bergson to modify his understanding of duration to insist on ideals of freedom and justice that are prior to life and in some instances direct their ends.[50] In this modification, Bergson shares with Valle-Inclán a belief that although qualitative experience is not determined by concrete ends, it is subject to the ethical considerations that shape life. As we will see below, these ethical considerations allow each author to confront the mechanization of warfare in World War I, arguing that Allied forces, the French in particular, are able to control new technology as opposed to being controlled by it.

In a 1914 lecture 'The Meaning of War: Life and Matter in Conflict', Bergson responds to German misappropriation of his theories by contrasting French forces, which he aligns with 'life', and German forces, which are aligned with 'matter'. Bergson notes the technological advances of the nineteenth century that 'had equipped man in less than fifty years with more tools than he had made during the thousands of years he had lived' and posits that each new machine becomes an 'artificial organ' which extends the 'natural organs'. Although this mechanical extension increases the human body's capabilities, it does not similarly increase its spirit, creating 'moral, social, international' disparities. Claiming that the French nation has attempted to address the disproportion through a corresponding inculcation of virtues like liberty, fraternity, and justice, allowing for what Bergson terms the 'spiritualization of matter', the German nation capitalized on technology's 'mechanization of spirit' to create a system in which human beings, instead of embracing 'harmonious diversity, as *persons* may do [...] fall to the uniformity of *things*' that 'mechanically obey a word of command mechanically transmitted'.[51] Confronting the mechanization of warfare that made World War I destructive in a way that had not been experienced previously, Bergson understands the Germans to be controlled by this

within a melody to explain the German misappropriation of Bergson. Although German authors claimed to be following Bergson when they argued that war allowed for the creation of 'a mystical experience of dynamic inclusive oneness', Jones argues that this position ignores Bergson's 'deliberately ambiguous conception of oneness [that] puts the "uni" or singular on the same ontological footing as the universal or all-embracing'. Like a melody in which 'each unfolding note holds its own as it is interpenetrated within the whole', Bergson's dynamic inclusive unity does not allow the individual to be effaced within 'total war mobilization' (p. 16).

50 Jones, 'Mysticism and War', p. 19.
51 Jones, 'Mysticism and War', p. 38. Italics in the original.

technology and the French to meet its power with renewed focus on the virtues that allow for regeneration.

In *Midnight*, Valle-Inclán shares Bergson's focus on the terrible devastation allowed for by the mechanization of war, describing in detail the extensive trenches lining the front that are flooded and filled with rats, trapping soldiers within, and, as mentioned above, the 'diverse modes of dying' introduced by new technologies: 'Machine guns attack with shots like lightning, they spread shells over a wide area, they level lines of soldiers' (p. 49); barbed wire is electrified (p. 46); aeroplanes 'carry their cargo of explosives to destroy, to burn, to kill' (p. 44). Even in descriptions that extoll the soldiers' heroism, the destructive capabilities of technological advances in warfare are acknowledged. Both authors posit, however, that even the devastation produced by the mechanization of warfare can allow for heroic action. In Bergson's terms, the 'mechanization of spirit' produced by technological advances can be countered by the 'spiritualization of matter'.

In the 1914 lecture, Bergson contrasts the virtues of 'naturally and purely heroic' French forces with German forces that have exploited mechanization:

> On the one side there was force spread out on the surface; on the other, there was force in the depths. On one side, mechanism, the manufactured article which cannot repair its own injuries; on the other, life, the power of creation which makes and remakes itself at every instant. On one side, that which uses itself up; on the other, that which does not use itself up.[52]

In what Jones characterizes as a fundamental extension of his theory of duration, Bergson argues in the context of World War I that life 'can only be sustained by ideals of freedom and justice higher than the life force itself'.[53] When confronted by World War I, Bergson modifies his theory to incorporate 'explicitly humanistic ends', making it 'more teleologic and transcendent than it had been'.[54] In *Midnight* we find a similar modification in the conception of astral vision. As we have seen, Valle-Inclán announces before leaving for the front that the view of a witness can only be partial, an account of a 'few grenades that fall here or there', and that his eventual war chronicle will express a 'view from

52 Henri Bergson, *The Meaning of the War: Life and Matter in Conflict*, ed. by H. Wilden Carr (T. Fisher Unwin, 1915), p. 37.
53 Jones, 'Mysticism and War', p. 19.
54 Jones, 'Mysticism and War', p. 19.

the stars'. We have also seen that Valle-Inclán's experiences at the front documented in his notebook record his observations as witness. Both perspectives are included in *Midnight*, resulting in a doubled narrator whose perspective, both mythic and documentary, creates the tension in the novel noted by Dougherty. It is as though the previous conception for the text theorized in *The Lamp of Marvels* and announced before leaving for France is met by the staggering experience of Valle-Inclán at the front and also incorporated into *Midnight: Astral Vision of a Moment of War*. The layering of the witness's perspective within astral vision, a perspective which, finally, is necessarily part of the mosaic created by the novel, creates an unresolved dialogism. *Midnight* moves back and forth between two perspectives — that of witness and that of Seer — to create an uneasy harmony of opposites that asks the reader to put in conversation the documentary and mythic, the perspective of the individual and that of astral vision.

The final third of *Midnight* presents striking examples of the movement between the perspectives of witness and Seer and the complex harmony of opposites that they produce. As discussed above, in Chapter 33 the narrator presents a mythification of war, extolling its regenerative potential and ability to unite a people:

> The soul of a people is eternal because of war. Generative desire is rekindled by it like a torch in a wind that strives to put it out. Only the threat of death perpetuates earthly forms, only death makes the world divine. (p. 67)

This mythification of war, however, is followed by a chapter focalized through the witness's perspective in which the technology of war denies heroism: German troops are 'crushed' by French grenades, the 'lizard-like flames' of machine guns rip through the shadows, French artillery bombards a field to cut off reinforcements (p. 68). Technological tools, as opposed to French soldiers, are identified as actors. In this context, the German soldiers are reduced to 'dispirited oxen' begging for their lives, but it is difficult to see how the mechanization of war and its effect on real bodies support a claim to French heroism or the regenerative effects on the 'soul of a people'.

If in these two chapters of *Midnight* the focus moves from astral vision to the perspective of a witness, this process is reversed in the final two chapters of the novel as the perspective of the witness returns to astral vision. The penultimate chapter makes clear that the witness's experience is also capable of mythologization, demonstrating that even within the devastation of World War I, individual actors or the actions of a collective — French soldiers in this instance — can infuse mechanized warfare with heroism. Comparing the field of battle 'at the apex of night and day' to the Catalaunian Plains in which the Romans defeated the Huns, the narrator focusses on the celebrated French general Henri Gouraud as he reviews the troops: 'He has an amputated arm and a face hardened by the sun, an exalted and mystic look, full of the blue light of sacred audacity'. Bearing the imprint of his particular experience of war, the General also transcends that experience: 'The tattered flags and that one-armed soldier damaged by the war form a unified and exemplary emotion'. The narrator concludes as the General awards the Legion of Honour to victorious troops: 'A religious emotion covers the great plain, and ancient shadows offer their laurels to the young heroes of divine France' (p. 72). This view gives way in the final chapter of the novel to that of a panoramic sweep of encampments at 'Ypres and Arras, Verdun and Reims, Thann and Metzeral' (p. 73). As we have seen, the narrator first documents the actions of soldiers in their encampments, distances his vision to record the movements of convoys heading to the next site of battle, and finally, from the perspective of astral vision, records the effects of war in 'a succession of desolate images, uninterrupted from the north coast to the Alsatian Mountains' (p. 73). General Gouraud and French heroism disappear, and the reader is left not with a mythification of war but with its destructive power and desolation.

The dialogism exemplified in this sequence of chapters is central to Valle-Inclán's aesthetics as laid out in *The Lamp of Marvels*. Seeking aesthetic quietude, the product of contemplation that breaks free from automatic response and action to allow one to become a centre of experiences viewed outside of temporal and spatial limits, Valle-Inclán asks his reader to pause, to put opposing perspectives in dialogue to create a harmony of opposites which is not a synthesis of these perspectives but rather allows each to exist with its full force, creating a type of simultaneity even as each perspective unfolds spatially in writing.

The 'Brief Notice' includes a reference to a general studying his map as a metaphor for astral vision: distinguishing the perspective of the general from that of the soldier fighting in the trenches, the narrator posits that the general would have a 'vision, an emotion, and a conception of the war distinct in every sense from that of the wretched witness who is subjected to the geometric laws of corporeal and mortal matter' (p. 39). Pointing to the distinction between qualitative and quantitative temporal experience, the tension produced by the view of the general and that of the witness make clear that an account that claims to be 'a collective vision [...] of all people who were in the war and saw at the same time all its settings, all its occurrences' (p. 40) is neither simply a glorification of the general and his more comprehensive perspective nor the partial view of the soldier whose body inscribes war's terrible effects, but exists as an uneasy tension that recognizes the force of both perspectives. The mutilated body of General Gouraud, which both inscribes war's devastating effects and gives these effects heroic meaning, stands as emblem to the contradictory forces at play in modern war.

The dialogism of Valle-Inclán's *Midnight* denies easy resolution, demanding a reader's active attention to bring opposing perspectives into the same interpretive field. This dual perspective presents not simply a mythification of war nor its condemnation but both, as the narrator moves across the spatial expanse and condensed temporal sphere. The product neither of a distanced narrator nor a partial witness but rather built on the uneasy rapprochement between both perspectives, the novel asks the reader to hold opposing views simultaneously.

The novel's dialogism, in this sense, reflects the tension between quantitative and qualitative temporal systems of interest to Henri Bergson, and between meditative and contemplative paths to knowledge introduced by Valle-Inclán in *The Lamp of Marvels*, identifying the author's solution to the problem of how to express perspectivism, simultaneity, and intuition in a written language that develops sequentially, fragmenting qualitative experience in the act of writing. Valle-Inclán cannot, finally, transcend the tool of his art, but the unresolved dialogism that characterizes *Midnight* — and, I would argue, his literary corpus in general — demands that his readers put opposing forces, like the temporalities we find here, in conversation to represent a more complex whole. Like the sentence that moves across the page in a fragmented approximation of lived experience, we are witnesses limited in the perception of our actions and those of others; but, as Bergson and Valle-Inclán argue, we are also capable of intuitions of qualitative experience that move outside of this fragmented real. We experience the world through our bodies, through action in the world, but we give meaning to these partial actions through a glimpse of the whole created through art and allowed for by quietism and aesthetic contemplation.

TRANSLATOR'S NOTE

THE SOURCE for this translation of *La media noche: visión estelar de un momento de guerra* is the edition by Bénédicte Vauthier and Margarita Santos Zas (Universidad de Santiago Press, 2017). Their edition glosses several words in Gallego, the language of Valle-Inclán's home region in the north-west of Spain, for which I am most grateful and which I note in the translation. Throughout, I have followed Valle-Inclán's non-standard capitalization and punctuation, understanding their use to be exploited by the author for their expressive potential. To suggest that the action occurs as the narrative is written, the text is largely composed in the present tense; the few shifts to past tense are indicated in the notes.

For clarity, I use the English words for place names. Valle-Inclán uses *Boche* and *Peludo* to refer to German and French infantrymen, respectively. The former derives from the French slang *tête de caboche* ('cabbage head'), and the latter is the Spanish translation of the French word *poilu* ('hairy'). Given their common use in English to refer to German and French soldiers in World War I, I use the French terms *Boche* and *Poilu* in the translation.

A major challenge for a translator of Valle-Inclán is to reproduce the internal rhythm that characterizes his prose. I am aware that my translation does not do justice to this component of the text, but I have attempted, when possible, to give some sense of its richness though the repetition of anchoring descriptions (e.g. 'the moon sails through skies of bright stars' (pp. 43, 44)) and the use of iterative lists, typically expressed in groups of three verbal phrases or adjectives. Valle-Inclán creates a wealth of similes and metaphors to describe the horrors of what the narrator sees. Although I have translated these literally to give as strong a sense as possible of their strangeness (e.g. the force of cannon fire 'opens up the air with that drawn-out and profound cry of pain that cats have when giving birth' (p. 49)), at other points in the text I have eschewed literal translation to protect the fluidity of the prose. These choices have been guided, always, by the desire to provide an English-speaking audience with as compelling a rendition as possible of Valle-Inclán's haunting 'moment of war'.

MIDNIGHT

ASTRAL VISION OF A
MOMENT OF WAR

ON LAS DOCE
DE LA NO-
CHE. La luna
navega por cie-
los de claras es-
trellas, por cie-
los azules, por
cielos nebulo-
sos. Desde los
bosques montañeros de la región alsaciana,
hasta la costa brava del mar norteño, se ace-
chan dos ejércitos agazapados en los fosos de

11

FIG. 3. Opening of Chapter 1 from *La media noche* (Imprenta Clásica Española, 1917). Image courtesy of *Cátedra Valle-Inclán*.

BRIEF NOTICE

M Y PURPOSE was to condense into a book the various and diverse occurrences of a day at war in France. When writing about war, the narrator, who was once a witness, provides a purely random chronology born of the human and geometric limitations that prohibit us from being in more than one place at the same time. And like anyone who must take many days to traverse the enormous battle-front stretching from the Alsatian Mountains down to the seacoast, the narrator adjusts the war and its unforeseen events to the measure of his own stride: Battles begin when his eyes begin to see them: The terrible sound of the war stops when he moves away from its tragic settings and returns when he comes closer.[1] All stories are limited by the geometry of the narrator's position. But he who could be in various places at one and the same time, as the Theosophists claim about Hindu mystics, and characters in novels say of Cagliostro who, when banished from Paris, exited simultaneously from all entrances to the city, certainly would have a vision, an emotion, and a conception of the war distinct in every sense from that of the wretched witness who is subjected to the geometric laws of corporeal and mortal matter. Between one mode and the other would be the same distinction as that between the view of the soldier who fights in the trenches and the general who follows the battle hunched over a map. This preternatural intuition of its settings and occurrences, this comprehension that seems to be outside of space and time, is not, however, foreign to literature, and one can even claim that it is the origin of primitive poems, religious vessels in which scattered voices and scattered stories have been conjoined, at the end of centuries, into the greatest story, or sign of all, in a supreme, almost infinite vision of the infinite eyes that close the circle. When the soldiers from France return to their villages, and the blind wander down paths with their guides, and those who don't have legs beg at the doors of churches, and one-armed amputees run

1 Valle-Inclán employs nonstandard punctuation for expressive purposes. Here, capitalization of the word following the colon suggests the gaze of a witness distracted by the 'unforeseen events' referenced in the previous sentence.

from place to place in the happy role of go-betweens; when at the family hearth the dead are named and prayed for, each mouth will have a different story and the stories will number hundreds of thousands, an expression of many other visions that in the end will be distilled into one vision, a sign of all things. Then the poor gaze of the soldier will dissolve to create a collective vision, the vision of all people who were in the war and saw at the same time all its settings, all its occurrences. The circle, upon closing, engenders its centre and out of this cyclical vision the poet is born who deserves to be called Seer.

I, clumsy and vain, wanted to be at the centre and to have an astral vision of the war, outside of geometry and chronology, as if my soul, already disembodied, were looking at the earth from a star. I have failed in my resolve. On this occasion my Indian drug denied me its marvellous outpouring. The pages that now come to light are no more than the stammering of a dreamed ideal. I will return to France and to the battle-front to refine my emotions, and perhaps I still might achieve that arrogant project of writing the visions and emotions of A DAY AT WAR.[2]

V.-I.

2 *A Day at War* is also the title of the fictionalized chronicle of Valle-Inclán's experience at the Western Front that was published serially in the Madrid newspaper *El Imparcial* between October 1916 and February 1917.

I lit the lamp at the edge of midnight. I placed myself in front of it, and my shadow covered the wall. I opened the book and spelled the words that disembody a soul wanting to look at the world outside of geometry. After, I put out the lamp and went to sleep on the ground with my arms crossed as the book directs. Artephius, Astrologer of Syracuse, wrote this book, named in Latin CLAVIS MAIORIS SAPIENTIAE.[3]

---

3 *Clavis maioris sapientiae* ('The Key to Greater Wisdom') is attributed to Artephius (*c.* 1150), although the identity of the historical figure is an open question. A thirteenth-century copy confirms that the text was first written in Arabic.

Chapter I

IT IS MIDNIGHT. The moon sails through skies of bright stars, through blue skies, through cloudy skies. From the mountainous woods of Alsace to the wild coast of the North Sea, two armies lie in wait, crouched in entrenchments that smell like death, as in a hyena's cage.[4] The French, son of the Latin wolf, and the barbarian German, bastard of all tradition, are once again at war. The defence lines stretch two hundred leagues, from the sea's cliffs to the mountains that dominate the green plains of the Rhine. Hundreds of leagues, and only the stars' eyes can see them fight at the same time, at the two tail ends of this long line, every hour filled with the flash of gunpowder and the thunder of cannon rolling through the sky.

Chapter II

THE TRENCHES are muddy and narrow ditches. They are swamped by yellowish waters from storms and floods. One slips while walking. Mice run lively along the inclines, water-loving rats scurry through the muddy bottom, and gusts of wind bring the cold stench of carrion. The trenchers have dug wide shelters into the slopes where squads of soldiers take refuge, and silos with lookouts are concealed among stones and branches in places favourable for monitoring. From these watch towers, enemy lines are discovered and artillerymen, communicating by telephone, order cannon, always placed behind the first defensive line, to fire. In front of the two enemy trenches lie thickets of barbed wire and ditches where the dead from the last few days rot on top of the skinned bones of those who fell in the first days of the invasion. The surrounding land looks like it has been ploughed. Shrapnel has cut down trees and burned grass. From the bottom of the trenches, rockets emerge with red, green, and white lights exploding in the dark night, briefly illuminating that vast battlefield. An alert sounds from the cliffs of the North Sea to the mountainous forests that trace the Rhine.

4 A map with all place names referenced in the text can be found on page 11.

Chapter III

IN THE NIGHT-TIME shadows, long convoys roll along, carrying ammunition to the front line. Rockets from the trenches open their roses
in the air, searchlights explore the battlefield and light up forests and
hills in the distance. Suddenly, they show the remains of a town in ruins,
burned and sacked, while in the flash of light produced by the searchlight,[5] a dog without his master runs, limping, along the roadway. At the
edge of the forest, rows and rows of unmoving trucks await their orders,
with soldiers from the convoy resting at the side of the road, smoking
pipes filled with Belgian tobacco. Cannon are heard, at times slowly, at
times in waves of fire, and the soldiers, almost indifferent, briefly con-
jecture. A cyclist arrives, persistently sounding a bell: He brings orders
that the sergeant makes out by a lantern's light, and the convoy gets
moving. All of the roads used by the rearguard feel the weight of ammunition trucks that, accompanied by veteran soldiers, bumble along
with the grating sound of iron. They move with headlights out, inde-
terminate forms under the stars, at times submerged in the trees' shadows and at other times standing out in black lines along a chalky and
bare roadway. There are so many that they cannot be counted, there are
hundreds and hundreds. They roll towards the trenches slowly, heavily.
When they pass near a village, dogs bark and roosters crow.

Chapter IV

AND THE MOON sails through skies of bright stars, through blue
skies, through stormy skies: Over the two hundred leagues of muddy
trenches, rockets open their roses, searchlights tremble, and in the
shadows, aeroplanes carry their cargo of explosives to destroy, to burn,
to kill... Cheerful pilots occupy the cockpits, crazed with airborne vertigo, like heroes from old tragedies crazed with erotic vertigo. Dressed
in furs, with large, round glasses and round, leather helmets, they
have an embryonic form and darkly evoke scientific monsters. They
fly against the wind and with the wind, the stars tell them their path.
Some go blindly through cloudy hollows, others soar above the smoke

5 Valle-Inclán uses the Gallego word 'lostrego' ('flash of lightning'), without the
accent on the first *o* that is its typical spelling, to refer to the effect produced by the
searchlight's beam.

and flames, others go by moonlight, stretching out in squadrons. That one foundering among waves of water and sea winds is from an English airfield in Picardy. And those that return and land in silence are French: There were seven that left at dusk and now there are no more than five: Behind them burns a train full of German soldiers. The pilots jump to the grass and move away, numb, while soldiers with lanterns push the planes into sheds and pour buckets of water on overheated motors. It is an aviation field at the rear of the battlefield on a flat expanse covered with grasses. Light tents, large sheds, lean-tos, and tack rooms make a ring on the grass that is the colour of night and fades into it: Only the moon highlights their silhouettes when it sails through clear, starry skies.

Chapter V

HAIL AND GALES in the Alsatian and Vosges Mountains. — The cock has already crowed twice. — The trenches have a white crest, and, hidden in them, dressed in furs like shepherds, guards spy on the enemy camp, barely leaning out across the snow-covered barricade. There is slow shelling, with long and linked resonance. The beam from a searchlight flies over the peaks, arrives at the bottom of the woods, lights the trunks of silver firs and the white slope of trenches where soldiers move quickly in Indian file to reinforce the defences of Hartmannswillerkopf. — *Le Vieil Armand* in the slang of the Poilus.[6] — Above the shroud of snow, rockets open out into many coloured roses. Between Thann and Metzeral a burst of enemy fire has begun, and in monitoring posts, dogs watch, crouched beside the soldiers.

Chapter VI

AT THE TOP of the mountain, the squad sergeant chooses two scouts: They leave cautiously, creeping along the snow, sinking into the night. The German trench, thatched and defended by a thorny web of wire, is on the other side of a glade, no more than one hundred steps away.

6 *Poilus*, the French word for 'hairy', was used during World War I to refer to French infantrymen. The original uses the Spanish translation, 'los peludos'. The Spanish 'El Viejo Armando' is used in the original to refer to the strategic observation post.

Great bullets cross whistling and, from time to time, a silver fir falls
to earth with the dull murmur of a surging sea. Soldiers run in small
groups, their heads turned, their shoulders raised. Another trunk creaks.
The shrapnel is mowing down the forest: Flames ignite where a bomb
falls. The two scouts drag themselves cautiously and, when the flash of
a searchlight lights up the field, they flatten themselves:[7] Shuddering,
they step over a pile of cadavers half buried in the snow: When they
take a step, they seem to absorb the bodies under their heels. The two
scouts cross over the dead, carrying their smell with them: Now they
touch the wire fence, and at that moment a violent shock throws them
through the air, their clothes on fire: The cartridges that they carry in
their belts explode like a rocket blast: They fall burning, like two effigies. A blue flame comes out of their helmets. From their trenches, the
French soldiers look on in pain. In the Langenfeldkopf Observatory, a
lieutenant murmurs, speaking with his colleague:

— The Boches have reinforced their defences with an electric cable,
imitating what we did in Indochina.[8]

Chapter VII

TAKING ADVANTAGE of the night's darkness, the Germans advance to
the defences of the French. Suddenly a dog's bark gives the alert, and a
searchlight exposes them crawling along the snow, their formation broken and very spread out. The French open fire. In a unanimous surge,
the Germans rise up and run towards enemy lines throwing hand grenades. When some fall, others replace them: They pull themselves up,
they fight in waves. The French open fire from defensive shelters. In a
few moments, only seventy from an advanced party of alpine veterans
remain unharmed. Grenades fall in the trenches. Telephone wires are
broken, and two soldiers volunteer to fix the break: A grenade explodes,
and one falls on the other: They twist tenderly towards each other, without horror, like two brothers who kiss. The lieutenant from the second

---

7 Valle-Inclán again employs the Gallego word 'lostrego' (again without the ac-
cented first *o*).

8 *Boche* is a disparaging term derived from the French phrase *tête de caboche* ('cabbage head') and used by Allied forces to refer to German soldiers. The reference appears to indicate French colonization of Indochina, beginning with Napoleon III's
invasion in 1858. The region was consolidated as the French Indochinese Union
in 1887.

company writes a message from inside a telephone sentry booth. Shouts are heard from Germans who have penetrated the trenches. The lieutenant folds the paper and fastens it under the collar of a dog that waits, wagging his tail: He pets him, takes him outside and shows him the trail. The dog takes off in a flash. The lieutenant takes a few steps and trips over a wounded man fallen at the bottom of the trench. Further away, another soldier bandages his forehead. Lieutenant Breal encourages them with his great voice: 'Long live France! Up with the dead!'[9]

And the dead rise up, and there is a great shift in that ditch full of darkness, of mud, of chaos. Two French machine guns open fire upon the dry, vacant land through which the Germans advance. Their shots attack methodically in a mathematical expression indifferent and cruel to men. Through the snowy forest, the dog's shadow flees: He runs along the side of a ditch, he enters a path where many vehicles wait in line: He appears and disappears: He jumps to escape the branch of a fir tree fallen in the road: He runs with his belly to the ground: Under the searchlights, he crouches like the soldiers. He is seen again along the side of a ditch, follows the trail, descends a slope to its bottom and, wagging his tail, enters a casemate.[10] Two officers write by the pointed light of an oil lamp, and the dog, prancing, comes between them, paws on the table. Lieutenant Russell pets him and takes out the message hidden in his collar. He begins to read it, and the other officer pronounces it syllable by syllable into the telephone:

— Brigade Command Headquarters. — Transmission from Lieutenant Breal. — 2nd Company of Alpine Hunters. — In a sudden attack, German forces have penetrated our defences. I am holding on with the men who remain, but I need help urgently. I have the command due to the disappearance of Captain Douchesne. — Lieutenant Breal.

Chapter VIII

BETWEEN THANN and Metzeral, shelling periodically heats up, but then falls into a stubborn and slow rhythm. The two enemy trenches wander through black forests and echoing ravines, sometimes tumbling downwards, sometimes moving up to the summit. Trunks of fir

9 The Spanish is '¡Arriba los Muertos!', which appears here in its literal translation to protect the response in the next paragraph: 'And the dead rise up'.
10 A casemate is a fortified structure used to store ammunitions and to shelter troops.

trees split, groaning and bowing under the storm of snow and shrapnel, branches block the roads. Metzeral is burning and a gleam of flames runs over the river: On each bank, houses are red, smoking skeletons: Walls and roofs fall with a dull thud. The inferno at Metzeral has blazed nightly since the beginning of the war. Women and children take refuge in church porticos, under broken arcades. Farm cows wander, lost, their bells ringing. In the abandoned streets, chests, beds, and clothes pile up. A couple with two children watch their house burn, sheltered amidst the ruins of other houses. The man holds the younger child in his arms, and the woman cries with her fingers entwined in the child's mop of hair. The infant complains with a whimper, and the father watches him without speaking, his eyes full of sadness. At his side, face up in a basket, a little girl sleeps: The father has covered her with his jacket, and her feet, wearing clogs and blue stockings, stick out. The mother suddenly gets up and uncovers the pale face of the infant.

— He's dying! He's dying! Don't you see that he's dying? We've lost our son!

The man is silent, and the woman looks at her husband:

— How can you keep holding him... You must be dead tired. Give him to me!

The man shakes his head. Then the woman cries:

— This war is a horror! We were so happy!

The little girl moves under the jacket, jumps up startled, screaming:

— Our baby died! Our baby died!

The father whispers weakly:

— Not yet!

The infant's sad whimper also responds. The mother grabs the child from the arms of his father: The infant screws up his eyes, trembles, and a thin thread of dark blood trickles from his finely shaped nose. His sister continues to shout:

— Our baby died! Our baby died!

The father takes her in his arms and presses his face against hers.

— Be quiet, my child! Be quiet!

The little girl understands, and stifling her sobs, kisses gently, gently, the beard of her father. But then she sighs again:

— Our baby died!

The mother begins:

— God took him! God took him! God took him!

She has a stubborn expression and dry eyes. With two fingers she closes the rigid eyelids of her dead child. Alpine scouts file by, heading to the trenches, they pass by without seeing them, bowed under the snowstorm. The roof of a house falls in, and in the deserted street the clip-clop of lost cows reverberates with the bong, bong of cowbells. The shelling, stubborn and slow, does not cease between the two infernos that are Thann and Metzeral.

Chapter IX

ECHOES OF WAR are linked from the north coast to the Alsatian Mountains! Flames emerge from the roar of bombs: The harvest burns, and overwhelms villages, and cities that cry when cathedral towers collapse. Thousands and thousands of soldiers fall in the great nocturnal battle and lie rigid and cold under shivering stars. Suddenly, squadrons of soldiers appear: At times breaking into two groups to look for an attack on the flank, at times under a bomb that bursts and opens a gap in the ranks like in the strong walls of a castle. Machine guns attack with shots like lightning, they spread shells over a wide area, they level lines of soldiers: Some fall like effigies, grotesquely folding their legs; others open their arms and are flattened against the ground; others bend slowly onto the shoulder of a comrade. And among such diverse modes of dying, the wounded drag themselves, pressing together torn flesh, feeling warm blood flow through their fingers, eyes wide with the horror of being taken prisoner. Thousands of cannon fire in succession, and the force of large projectiles opens up the air with that drawn-out and profound cry of pain that cats have when giving birth.

Along roads dug by trenchers that reach the line of fire, orderlies carry the wounded. First aid is given in the trenches, in the shelter of deep casemates that have pools of blood on their earthen floors and air permeated with the smell of chloroform. At the shoulder of the road, in the protection of forests and hills, trucks from the Red Cross wait immobile, in long lines. Ambulances are in the rearguard, distributed among granaries and farm stables, in rooms of castles, in cafés with scratched mirrors and nets for the flies, in the cellars of towns that are still burning. The pain of the war shakes and restores the soul of France!

Chapter X

THICK FOG on the sea-coast. — The cock has already crowed twice. — Stars tremble over the flooded plain of Flanders. In an estuary near Veurne, sailors disembark, forming the vanguard. Sea winds blow, and the undertow drags bruised and swollen cadavers of German soldiers towards the shore: A wave carries them in on its foamy crest, another wave swamps them. Their black, flooded boots are buried in the sand, their large, swollen bodies are knocked down with a dull thud. A squad of sailors who cordons off the beach is silent, looking at the choppy and bottomless horizon. They are fishermen from Normandy and Brittany, gullible young men with pale eyes, childlike souls who are brave on the water, open to miracles, and afraid of the dead. Many pray in a low voice, remembering apparitions in the cemeteries and pine forests of their villages; others drink aguardiente and smoke pipes;[11] perhaps another tries to sing. The moon sails through the clouds, and the swollen bodies of Boches come and go with the undertow.

Chapter XI

A SHIP'S LIEUTENANT, accompanied by a constable, follows the guard down the shore. He greets the sailors, and all, like children, feel the fear of the dead that made them pray and sing dissipate in the presence of their leader. An artillery corporal steps out of line, raises his hand in salute, drawing attention to himself:

— With permission, Lieutenant. Will you allow us to rig them up with sails?

And he signals the cadavers of the German soldiers run aground on the beach. The lieutenant understands and smiles:

— Wouldn't it be better to bury them?

— Unless you command otherwise, Lieutenant, it's better to rig them up with sails and let the wind take them.

The group of sailors cries in response:

— Let the wind take them! Let the wind take them!...

They are grave cries, fearful and astonished: Their rumbling is something like a prayer. A sailor from the Breton coast crosses himself:

11 Aguardiente is Spanish moonshine liquor. Because of this word's generally accepted use, I have used it instead of the translation 'firewater'.

— The living and the dead shouldn't sleep together!

The officer gestures with indifference:

— Then let the wind take them.

— At your order, Lieutenant!

The group of sailors disperses on the beach, one group saying quietly to another:

— Come on! Rig them up with sails.

Someone asks:

— And the Lieutenant?

— It's the Lieutenant who orders it.

Chapter XII

THE SAILORS roll up their pants and enter, splashing, the phosphorescent water. Along the beach float more than one hundred inflated and swollen German bodies. There is one that doesn't have a head; others display purplish bruises, almost black, on their stomach or legs. The task of making sails of poles and tent canvases begins. Using boat hooks, they make holes in the water-logged flesh and pound in shafts where they will put the tarps. Then, both superstitious and skilled, they push them until they find a breeze: They twist the sail so that the wind will fill it, and, by the heel or by the neck, they tie up the ropes. The dead move away from the beach like a fleet of feluccas:[12] They line up under the moon, and head out towards the ocean horizon, pushed by the cool breeze that blows from the third quadrant. A wave of happiness passes over those infantile and gullible souls. A cabin boy, cap in hand and the light of the stars in his fervent eyes, exclaims in his old Celtic language:[13]

— Mother of God! I am no longer afraid of the dead!

Chapter XIII

SLOW SHELLING on the side of Ypres. A stream of mud flows at the bottom of the trench; guards huddle together with their rifles leaning against the slope; small squads of soldiers doze in dugout shelters along

---

12 A felucca is a traditional wooden sailing boat with one or two sails that was commonly used in the Red Sea and Eastern Mediterranean.

13 Although the narrator reports that the subsequent line is spoken in an 'old Celtic language', it appears in Spanish in the text.

the trench. From time to time, the steps of an officer moving through the line stop at the entrance:

— Look alive, boys!

The soldiers surge in the shadows, they respond as a gang, they feel blindly for their guns. The officer moves away, continuing along the advance line. Many Poilus, covered by waterproof canvas, rest at the bottom of the trenches with their heads reclining on boxes of hand grenades. The officer moves slowly among them, feeling his way with a stick. All of a sudden, a dozing guard startles awake and fires his gun. The alarm sounds. There are sudden gunshots; rockets soar and the Poilus who rest in the back of trenches get up, reaching for boxes of grenades. The fire slowly extinguishes; the line returns to the shadows, shaken and vigilant, in a tense waiting that is more wearying than battle.

Chapter XIV

THE ASHEN PLAIN is without end at night, and, when the light of the moon clears the haze, it reveals the spectre of a bombed-out city: The city of Arras. Black and gutted houses smoke; the cathedral is a mountain of rubble; piles of stone spill onto four streets, blocking them: Mutilated rosettes and crosses, gargoyles and columns appear among the ruins. Bombs fall and open large hollows in Spanish-style patios, and many houses, doors open and windows banging in the wind, display furnishings piled up in the gloomy recesses of entryways. A wagon pulls away: Its load of chests, dishes, and mattresses sways: A cradle perches on top. The city seems abandoned: There are places where houses are flattened and scattered over the ground like sandcastles built by children, and entire streets where the skeletons of buildings remain standing, but with their façades destroyed, revealing bourgeoise interiors and an anguished abandonment full of the shouts of women and cries of frightened children who cling to their skirts. In a narrow, steep street sheltered from the bombing, another wagon loads. A group of women kiss one another. The driver hurries them up, and those leaving climb in: A widow with two daughters, two pale girls, hair uncombed, teary-eyed. They arrived a little while ago, fleeing from Combles. Their father went to the war, and the two girls are pregnant by German soldiers.

Chapter XV

THE WAGON begins to move, and the three women cross themselves. A
little later, the mother dozes. The wagon moves along a roadway lit by
the moon: The girls look at the road with suspicion, raise the tarps, and,
with sad eyes, follow the red lights of planes that cross the sky like wan-
dering stars. They hear distant bombing and smell the humid fragrance
of hay. From time to time at the edge of the roadway they see a herd of
cattle appearing indistinctly like a giant smudge at the back of the pasture; at other times they see a village in ruin. The roadway lengthens
over the plain, infinitely lengthens: Large windmills with still blades,
erect, watch the road from distant hills. Farms are glimpsed through
hazy, black foliage; rays of light filter between the cracks of shutters,
and one imagines an interior filled with soldiers. One of the girls sticks
her head between the wagon tarps and asks the driver in a voice filled
with pain:
— Is there much further to go, friend?
The driver responds confusingly, with his pipe between his teeth:
— Less than at the beginning.
The girl barely smiles, closes her eyes, and presses down on her waist:
— My body is torn apart by pain!

Chapter XVI

ALL OF A SUDDEN, the wagon stops, still swaying, and the driver jumps
to the ground. Grumbling, he knocks his empty pipe against a wheel
tyre, and puts it in a pocket of his sheepskin jacket. The three women
look at one another, afraid. The mother questions the girls:
— My daughters, what's happening? Ay, what a bad dream! What a
bad dream! But what's happening?
The shepherd raises a tarp and takes a pole from the back of the
wagon:
— No need to be frightened, ladies! It's a dead horse.
The horse — rigid, black, enormous — was stretched out in the middle of the road, almost filling it from one side to the other. Its belly was
ripped open and its guts exposed in a pool of sticky blood. Putting the
pole in the belly and levering it against the ribcage, the driver moves

the horse to the side of the road. It is half buried in a ditch, with its neck twisted and four legs in the air:

— Poor beast!

The driver jumps onto the wagon seat and once again takes the reins. Like at the beginning of the journey, the three women make the sign of the cross and pray. They pass a squadron of Indian horsemen, their faces dark, their turbans black. There are long lines of immobile vehicles on the side of the road. Machine gun carriages, ammunition trucks, wagons filled with hay. There are too many to count. Two automobiles pass quickly, leaving a trail of dust and gasoline; they carry officers from General Headquarters. A new squadron of Indian horsemen, new trucks immobile on the side of the road, and a diffuse row of infantrymen, gloomy, hunched-over, silent: They lean on pike staves and carry packs. When crossing a village, the girls hear Scottish bagpipes. Two old farmers stop the wagon; the driver gives them the route order, and after reading it by the light of a lantern, they return it to him. The wagon starts moving again. One of the girls cannot stop crying out:

— Oh, Holy Virgin Mary!... My body is torn apart by pain!

Chapter XVII

Now fields covered with crosses appear on both sides of the road: Their arms grow larger in the misty haze that fills the night and forms a halo of light. A long row of bodies rests on the slope of the road: Four hoes dig and fill the air with the smell of overturned earth. A group of soldiers works to identify the cadavers, and their pale faces surge suddenly under the lantern's cone of light. A voice in the shadows speaks:

— Here is one that doesn't have a head!

And another voice further away questions:

— Is he a Zouave?[14]

— A Zouave.

— The head must have rolled away. I remember putting it on his stomach.

Amidst the fog and stars, the figures, the lights, and the voices loosely reconcile life and dreams. With the light from his lantern, an orderly searches the ditches along the road and shouts to those on the other side:

— I've got it!

14 A Zouave is an infantryman from French North Africa.

And he raises the truncated head, covered with dirt and blood. Another soldier drives his pickaxe into the side of a ditch that almost covers him, pulling himself out:

— This bed is ready for three more Boches!

The others respond from the road:

— Here they come!

They carry the dead by their feet and shoulders; their arms hang rigidly; their hands scrape the soil. The hoes rest, the frogs sing from the recesses of fields, and the dead go to the bottom of the ditch. A military chaplain blesses the ground. The soldiers remove their helmets and make the sign of the cross. The blurry silhouettes of two soldiers who tamp down the earth dance amidst the haze and the moon, and the orderly who recovered the truncated head cleans his hands, sticky with blood, in the grass. Then, scattered along the side of the road, the soldiers drink aguardiente to rid themselves of unhappy thoughts.

Chapter XVIII

THE WAGON STOPS at the entrance to the village of Saint-Denis in front of a hospital with three rows of equally sized windows. Many houses have caved-in roofs; others are partially demolished; acacia trees in the plaza also show effects of the bombardment, and many broken branches cover the road like a carpet. All of the windows in the hospital are without glass. The three women timidly enter the lobby, and a skirted nun, with a long veil and a large rosary swinging from her waist, comes to meet them. On seeing her, the two sisters begin to sob in extreme distress, and the nun takes them by the hand and leads them through a white corridor, lit at great intervals by small petroleum lamps. The Stations of the Cross unfold along the wall, and the vast silence of the holy house is broken by the cries of a woman in pain. The two girls, with handkerchiefs held to their faces, stifle their distress, and the nun speaks to them, consoling them in a soothing voice. The mother follows behind, stunned, shattered, exhausted. An errand girl carrying bed linens quickly passes by:

— Holy Virgin Mary!

— Conceived without sin!

She pushes the half-opened door at the end of the corridor, and, briefly, they glimpse another old nun, seated in a low chair, putting swaddling clothes on a newborn. The two sisters, tense and crying aloud, look at their mother and hug her. Gently pushing them, the nun leads them into a large room — white, square, cold by virtue of being clean and bare.

Chapter XIX

WHEN THE DOCTOR enters, the nun moves away and waits at the door, eyes lowered and hands folded. The doctor is an old, gaunt man with the passionate and eloquent expression of a great talker. He greets them upon entering:

— What ails these girls?

Then, seeing that they are upset, he murmurs with an appeasing and pleasant voice:

— Well, I already know what ails you! Don't worry, my daughters!

He sits near to the mother:

— First, we should speak.

The mother looks stubbornly at her folded hands and raises her eyebrows:

— Yes, sir, yes... You already know...?

— About all of it, children, about all... They say that it is part of war... A lie! Never have burning and rape been necessary to war. It is atavistic barbarity asserting itself... Men, still very close to their jungle ancestors, are revived by these great moments. The war exposes their true nature and puts it on display, like wine with drunkards.

One of the girls murmurs nervously:

— It is a hatred of France!

The doctor, full of sympathy, looks at her and reaches for her hand:

— It is a hatred of the classical world, my daughter. A foundling's hatred for those who have lineage.

That old, gaunt man, with sunken eyes hidden by long eyelids like those of an eagle, had a passionate sincerity in his voice that began to win the hearts of the three unfortunate women. The mother is white, heavy, her face reddened by tears: She reminds one of a shabby and mistreated doll destroyed by a child. Only the younger of the two daughters has her mother's features. Caroline, the older, is tall, thin, with a moonlike paleness and dark eyes loaded with sadness. Her smile, once full of grace, has not yet disappeared completely. She has wild hair, and when she moves it off her forehead, two marks of madness are visible near her temples. Enriqueta, the younger, is blonde, very childlike, and with a white and fine complexion that is chafed from crying. The doctor gets up, looks closely at the two girls, assesses them, and finally asks them to stand up. With a profound and serious look, he looks them over from top to bottom:

— Alright! I already know... At present it is not necessary to bother you more. Now you should rest. Tomorrow I will do a detailed examination...

The older of the girls lets herself fall into a chair, covering her face with her hands:

— Doctor, I don't want to have the child of these barbarians!... I don't want to carry this infection in me! If you do not free me from this disgrace, I will kill myself!

She ended her cries in a nervous attack,[15] screwing up her eyes, grinding her teeth, and jumping out of her chair into the arms of her mother and sister who had gone to hold her. She emerged from this state pale, haggard, contrite, speaking in a very tenuous voice filled with the helpless pain of a miserable life now over:

— To be born for this! To have lived for this!

Chapter XX

CLOSE TO DAWN, a convoy of wounded soldiers arrives. Forty Red Cross wagons stretch out under the mutilated trees. There isn't enough space, and Belgian nuns, refugees at the hospital from a French village, offer their rooms and beds white like altars to the Republican soldiers. Hallways overflow with the wounded. They lie on stretchers on both sides of the hallway, forming a *via dolorosa* filled with moans and drawn-out groans. Some of the more slightly wounded, pale and sleepy, their bandages splattered with blood and mud, rest on waiting room benches. The stairway is full of soldiers sleeping with packs beneath their heads: They wrap themselves in brown blankets, they exhale humid breath: They are raw recruits and so overwhelmed with fatigue that, on finding shelter, they throw down their packs and stretch out. — The hallways are full of movement, of voices, and of mud. The studs of heavy military boots leave their imprint in a path formed by two rows of stretchers. At the sound of footsteps, a hand, its paleness visible beneath mud and gunpowder, raises an oilcloth blanket:

— I'm dying of thirst! I'm dying of thirst!

15 The shift to past tense is in the original.

It is a feeble voice. The soldier's forehead is wrapped in gauze bandages with round patches of fresh blood, and his face disappears under the bandages. Weak moans escape from other stretchers, and from still others feverish words, death rattles, delirious shouts; there are also some that are profoundly silent, like coffins. The moans, the cries, the chaotic speech unwinding without rest form a confused babel. One wounded soldier doesn't stop crying:

— The English! The English!

He shakes the stretcher and draws out his arms, his hands waving about:

— The English! The English!

And always the same, the same inexpressive stupor in his cry, the same dark thought going around and around like a millstone. It was more distressing to hear than a terrible scream.[16] Another wounded man cries out heroically; another laughs with great merriment:

— Don't leave, Juana! Listen, Juanita!... Ha, ha!... If you leave, I'll pinch you!

Chapter XXI

IN THE OPERATING ROOM, white and lit-up, doctors and nurses with aprons have no rest from washing wounds, staunching blood, tearing bandages. Alcohol lamps raise blue flames over marble tables; the assistants disinfect scissors and tweezers; chloroform, smelling of apples, saturates the air. Dr Verdier murmurs as he undresses a wounded man:

— We're overwhelmed, I'm afraid... We'll have to see about setting up the church because soon we'll be out of space here. And straw? Is there enough straw for pallets?

A great battle is being waged; distant and constant bombing is heard. Cavalry patrols, machine gun carriages, ammunition convoys escorted by infantry troops parade down the remaining street in the village, only to lose themselves in the fog that arrives from the south-east.

Chapter XXII

FOR MANY DAYS, the English and French have been bombing non-stop German lines in Flanders and Picardy. All rearguard roads are full of

---

16 The tense shift follows that of the original Spanish text.

wagons and troops: Automobiles from General Headquarters steadily
pass by. In some places, there is so much mud that soldiers are buried
in it up to their waists and wagons cannot move. Large convoys, pro-
tected by trees that stop the shrapnel, wait for hours and hours, de-
tained at the side of the road: Hours and hours, until the new route
order arrives. — The vast horizon line cracks with a flash of cannon,
there are so many that the flashes join together and seem like an enormous blink of an eye in the dark land. The armed forces disappear into
the silos of parapets, and on black plains now empty of men, the roar
from the cannon mouths has the magnificent, religious resonance of a
cataclysm's most elemental scream. Troops stationed in the rearguard
feel a unanimous impulse to run forwards: Soldiers open their hearts
to victory, and horses greet the hot smell of gunpowder with sensuous
neighing. In the middle of horror and death, a profound current of joy
runs through the French armed forces. It is a consciousness of resurrec-
tion. — Artillerymen, buried in casemates, regulate cannon fire with a
mathematic and devoted sensibility, like artisans who work the stones
on a temple. It is the religion of war, and since their souls are joined in
brotherhood, their words are brief: They communicate in silence by
virtue of a smile and light in their eyes: When leaning out of embra-
sures to contemplate grenade fire, they assume the radiant expression
appearing on the face of mystics in the presence of holy apparitions.

Chapter XXIII

BOMBS RAIN DOWN on German trenches, collapsing them, clearing
them out, levelling them: It is a cyclone of fire. And if Teuton artillery
responds with rage in some places, it is quiet in others, unable to cover
the Allies' extensive line of attack. The trenches' parapets are filled with
dead bodies, and astonished soldiers, drawing back from their leaders,
await the attack of enemy infantrymen with no plan in mind, indifferent to victory, indifferent to hope. They were once masters of power
and obscurely perceive that a superior power has been born contrary to
theirs, contrary to the destiny of Germany. A profound chasm opens in
those naïve and barbaric souls once filled with faith. The commanders
feel the quiet rebuff of the soldiers, their detachment from the invaded
land, a peaceful longing to return to their homes: And they get those
in the trenches drunk to revive their spirits and tie soldiers to machine
guns so they cannot desert, and the whip of officials who patrol the
frontline sounds continuously.

Chapter XXIV

AN ENORMOUS BATTLE CRY shakes all of Picardy. Small towns are filled with soldiers, with horses, with ammunition wagons: There are stands with hot coffee on street corners, and small inns along the road, illuminated by petroleum lamps, overflow with uniforms: Light from their pipes wavers in red reflection on their faces, clustered together at the counter in the misty smoke. From time to time, a soldier goes to the door, looks at the sky, and extends his hand to check the rain. Along the road, machine gun carriages, hay wagons, ammunition trucks, artillery wagons await their orders. Automobiles with officers pass by and are rapidly lost in the fog: Cyclists with their guns like pennants, panting and stubbornly peddling, and cavalry patrols, and squadrons of infantrymen pass by. Scottish bagpipes sing in the night; rockets open their roses in the air; searchlights scout fields, and vehicles begin to move, tearing up the roads. Three bonfires, three large bonfires, redden the plane: Three villages that the Germans, in retreat, have set on fire.

Chapter XXV

SOME ARTILLERYMEN sleep in the hay of a farm's stable, and the night watchman shouts, banging on the door:
— Order to depart! Order to depart!
Pulling the herd by their collars, they hitch them up in the darkness. It is raining. Ill-humoured artillerymen move like shadows from place to place:
— Nasty weather!
They stumble, they curse, they crack their whips against the horses' haunches. A voice questions:
— Does anyone know where we are going?
And another responds:
— To the Dance of the Sugared Almonds.[17]
What a stormy night!
The horses lengthen their necks, shaking their ears in the rain. In the darkness, men and beasts, each with a halo of fog, move with

17 The ambiguous expression may refer to a wedding tradition and initiates a thread of ironic comments by soldiers less than thrilled by marching to battle on a stormy night.

disembodied slowness. One cannot distinguish who speaks, and voices are vague, as if arriving from far away:

— Lousy weather and lousy war! When will this end!

— This will never end!

A soldier shouts furiously:

— Sooo!... The devil take this thief! Sooo, Fanfan![18]

Drivers on wagon seats loosen bridles and crack their whips. A squadron forms on the muddy road. A small stove glows on a street corner sheltered by a church, and an old woman sells coffee and aguardiente to soldiers, who, inclining over the necks of their horses, stretch out cups and canteens. The old woman goes from one to the other with her hand in a waist pouch full of loose change:

— Good luck, boys!

The battery moves down the pothole-filled road, amidst waves of rain and waves of wind that upset the horses' manes. The darkness is so dense that artillerymen seated on gun carriages cannot see the team in front of them, and the guide's silhouette is a faltering and unstable shadow. The soldiers remain silent, numb, and discouraged. From time to time, a grumble:

— Lousy weather!

— Lousy war!

— And it will never end!

— Only the women will stop it.

A soldier takes the lid off his aguardiente-filled canteen and offers it to the soldier next to him on the gun carriage. The other drinks:

— It's a leisurely trip! And where are the gentlemen taking us?

— Where we are not needed. When we get there, they'll order us to withdraw.

— If only the cars at General Headquarters would break down!

Gun carriages bounce along the potholes. Mud splatters the backs of artillerymen. Whips crack on the hind-quarters of horses galloping into wind and rain, their manes cresting in waves.

All along the line, there is suspicion-filled silence. The huff and puff of a train that spills its brilliant tail of sparks is heard in the stormy night sky.

---

18 'Fanfan' appears to be a reference to the traditional French hero Fanfan La Tulipe, a soldier who fought against the British in the Seven Years' War (1756–1763), antagonized his superiors, and got away with it due to his quick wit.

Chapter XXVI

THE ARGONNE FOREST! Wind and rain! God's awesome wind and rain!
A silent squad of French infantrymen advance in Indian file, sloshing
through mud in the trenches. The corporal leads the way with a muffled
lantern that opens waves of light in the blackness of the trench. They
are sixteen men, sad and numb, sixteen wills submissive to the destiny
of France. They advance through the flooded trench, slipping, falling,
getting up covered with muck, resigned to the wind, the rain, and death.
From time to time, they hear the clash of shovels and pickaxes amidst
the muffled whispers of their march. In some places, the foul smell of
rot makes their skin crawl. In others, German cannon fire has dug up
the earth to such an extent that not even the slightest trace of the trench
remains, and the soldiers are lost in a sea of mud. Tomín, the corporal of the squad, inspects the ground and in a low voice gives orders to
open the drain. The soldiers work with sombre resignation and a trace
of hatred for those who invade French lands: Those snub-nosed and
brutal soldiers, who sing like savages, fight drunk, tolerate an officer's
whip, are slaves in a land where there are still bloodlines and kings! For
the French soldiers, feelings of human dignity are rooted in a hatred of
hierarchies: The Marseillaise moves them to tears, and from old revolutions they have the sentimental idea of an almost forgotten melodrama
in which princes and kings are always traitors.

Chapter XXVII

THE SIXTEEN MEN in the squad work in silence: They are only a few
steps from the German line and the slightest murmur will give them
away: They open a ditch that in a few moments is again obstructed by
muddy water. Broken and twisted barbed wire rises out from the mud,
ripping up flesh, and they dig, tangled up in it. When rockets light the
sky, the Poilus stand still in the lake of mud. From time to time a stray
machine gun lets loose its thunder: The sound fades intermittently in
gusts of wind and rain, it has deep folds as if taking on the broken form
of the terrain: It is suddenly revealed and suddenly diminished with
a sound full of drama. The soldiers extend the ditch until it meets a
ravine, and the water rushes in a torrent. The form of the trench begins to take shape. Some bodies appear rooted in the bottom, and the

soldiers take them from the mud, lining them up on the slope. They dig up two machine guns twisted like wood shavings. The corporal shines his lantern into one of the shelters: The light flickers over the sleeping water, and startled rats scamper up the earthen wall, and a pair of black and swollen boots breaks the ray of light on the pool. The water makes a circle around them. The feet of the dead man sway slightly. The corporal whispers:

— Let's wait until morning to bail out the water.

An infantryman draws near and sticks his head in, observing from behind the corporal.

— It seems no one here was saved.

The corporal looks at him over his shoulder:

— The rats!

— Those men are already at rest!

— Well, you wouldn't change places with them... And in the end, if not today, tomorrow we'll be like this.

They move away, bent beneath the storm. They hear the sound of water going down the ravine. The soldier murmurs:

— If only the war would end!

— You, what family do you have over there?

— A wife and three children. And you?

— No one!

— Are you single?

— Divorced.

The corporal puts the lantern in the opening of another shelter. The light flickers over the black water. A sheep dog swims holding the arm of a sinking body in his teeth. They see a pale hand. The dog swims towards the light.

Chapter XXVIII

THE DAWN STARS turn pale and the replacement of troops along the battle-front begins. Columns of soldiers advance along hundreds of roads. Those going to the trenches earnestly smoke their pipes and avert their eyes from the battle, speak with innocent smiles, have faces burned from the cold and a serene look. Along the highways, one can make out large convoys: At times immobile, stretched out along bombed-out villages; at other times, rolling along; at still others, resting in the shade of a poplar grove. The soldiers returning from the trenches walk

in silence, dispersed stragglers covered with clay, their faces very pale and their eyes stunned beneath furrowed, obstinate brows. Forms reveal their contours in the indecisive light of dawn. With a great racket of grating iron, black trains laden with troops cross hazy bridges: They escape across the plains, appear and disappear among thickets, pant up tall embankments. Behind the enormous trench that curls from the sea to the Alsatian Mountains, bombed towns that are the tragic manifestation of war rise out of the night. Enclosed cities by serene rivers, villas near provincial roads, villages among fields display their ruins to the battlefield. Houses, black from fire, with the roof collapsed inside four thick walls and innards crumbling in rubble, are arid and heartbroken ruins. In many, the surrounding land is already full of nettles and lizards. Among burned and sacked towns, military cemeteries extend to the edge of roads. — Fields of crosses, humid fields whose sad and clear green is like the remote and musical emotion issuing from the divine lament of a lover! — Cemeteries mark battle lines, and French and German graves are dug at the same time. The hazy dawn thins out over the ruins, breaks up in the crosses, flies weightlessly over the enormous trench from the Alsatian Mountains to the Flemish coast, and in this ashen transition from night to day, the forms of the dead begin to show themselves. There are places where bodies are piled up, and others, many leagues long, filled with the song of birds, as if the killing were forgotten. This cold and grey moment when the soldier leaves the night's darkness and looks around at his dead comrades, the broken machine guns, the collapsed trench is the most distressing of the war. The troops return from the trenches to their lodgings with an expression of tragic madness. And to the innkeeper in front of the door where they stop to drink a cup of wine; and the old people working the fields; and the women leading covered wagons; to all who ask about the battle, they respond with the same obstinate gesture, with the same passionate voice:
— They will not pass!

Chapter XXIX

AT THIS SAME HOUR it is snowing and blizzard-like in the Alsatian Mountains, thick with fog near the sea, white with cold in Champagne... But in the two hundred leagues of swampy trenches, full of rats and flashes of light, where the Poilu shivers with aching hands on his gun, bombs burst and knock down the bulwarks, machine guns unleash their thunder, the deep echo of landmines unfolds. There are places full of fervour, rage, and tumult that suddenly are left in silence with long rows of dead crushed against the earth. Large flocks of crows swoop down under the dawn's sky. An injured man hidden in the brush moans, as does the one who drags himself along the side of the road, and the one covered in blood who lies on the slope of the trench, and those on stretchers who are pale with foreheads bandaged and eyes open. The patrols explore the countryside, and through the thousand paths that get to the line of fire, soldiers move in a spread-out, diffuse line. To avoid slipping in the mud, they support themselves on strong sticks, and orderlies come and go by different paths. In one casemate around a stove where water boils for coffee, officers converse about the war and women. They are young and have a smile full of an unconscious grace for life and death, like during the time of the Great Revolution.

Chapter XXX

IN THE REARGUARD, those at General Headquarters keep watch. The telephone rings continuously: Soldiers, covered in mud and the fog's condensation, arrive on bicycles: News from the battle-front is received, orders are transmitted, and officers hunch over, consulting large geographic maps. When they name the Germans, they do so without hatred and without arrogance, but with that intimate disdain that the Latin people had for foreigners. — For the French soul, harmonious and classic, the Teuton continues to be the barbarian. — Electric bells do not stop ringing, and everything is done slowly, with restraint, without nervousness. From time to time an officer, who salutes and stands at attention, appears in the doorway of the vast room: He comes from the darkness, from the mud, from the rain, and he brings a folder. The General shakes his hand and offers him a cup of hot coffee. After, and with the noble courtesy that is traditional in the French armed forces, he asks him to speak. And once again the bells, and the brief orders, and the waiting, the attentive waiting.

Chapter XXXI

ON THE GREAT PLAIN of Picardy, the battle heats up. Through the labyrinth of trenches dug to the rear of the first line and leading to it, squadrons of English and French infantrymen advance, running in Indian
file, slipping and splashing in the mud, longing to arrive. German
bombs sound, lighting the air in the fog's grey chaos, and burst, collapsing the embankments. Occasionally, the way is blocked, and the
troops scatter and march quickly, exposed under enemy fire. The vast
battlefield confronts them all at once, gloomy and profound, shaken
incessantly by the fire and thunder of cannon. Crouching, they once
again enter the labyrinth of trenches, and walk, buried in mud up to the
backs of their knees, but with new courage. Platoons of infantrymen
arrive at the frontline by diverse roads and from faraway places; the
labyrinthine ditches are a human anthill. On a slope providing a view
of the enemy camp, squads line up their guns and fire. Torpedoes, on
bursting, destroy bulwarks and bury men; they trace their slow curve
in the sky; they fall steaming; they open deep holes. And, at the back
of the field, the glow of three villages in flames burns against the black
sky. — A line of tragic women hugging their children, and of old people
raising their arms.

Chapter XXXII

AT THE EDGE of dawn, the Allied infantry launched itself out of the
trenches, assaulting German defences.[19] The soldiers run in wing formation with their heads low, made bold by artillery fire; they slip, fall,
slosh about, escape the trenches, get torn up by barbed wire. At times,
they disappear in sinkholes caused by shelling, submerging slowly, and
muddy water swirls around their helmets. The hole in the earth dug
by the shells is so deep that only their hands stick out, asking for help.
There are places that are true quaking bogs. German machine guns
open fire and entire rows of soldiers fall, as if bending in two. In the
middle of the cloud of smoke, some heroic soldiers continue advancing
quickly, grenades in hand. Columns of assault troops follow in waves:
The dead remain, crushed on the ground, half naked, their clothes torn

19 Valle-Inclán uses past tense at the beginning of this chapter to establish action
that occurs just prior to the witness's description.

away by the explosions: The wounded drag themselves along ditches, looking for a place to hide, and, finding safety, raise cries asking for help:

— Aren't I worth saving? Aren't I worth saving?

— A drop of water!

— Orderlies! Orderlies! Orderlies!

— And you're letting me die?

— Oh! Oh! Oh!

— Aren't I worth saving? Aren't I worth saving?

The fog is full of these lost voices, dulled by pain; but the wave of soldiers keeps crossing the plain, they run facing German trenches filled with the dead, and they throw their grenades and shout with the dramatic exhilaration of war. The memory of flames from villages blazing against the black sky passes in front of their eyes and covers their souls with a burst of magnificent rage.

— Boches! Barbarian Boches!

Chapter XXXIII

WHAT MAGNIFICENT FURY! What crashing and rebounding, what mythic strength demonstrated by the assault in the trenches! And what a blind impulse for life in this contest of pain and death! How the great battle breaks and splits into partial actions, in marches, in flanking actions, in surprises, until astral vision fades completely in the tumult of body on body, and finishes in a shout like the victorious cry of a rooster! But mathematic thought, stronger than life and death, remains immutable in all forms of battle; it governs the tumult of the trenches as well as artillery fire. All the diverse and unexpected actions that occur without warning find a harmonious link in this formidable accord. The war has an ideal architecture that only the eyes of the initiated can grasp and, thus, is full of telluric mystery and light. No other of men's creations better reveals a profound sense of landscape and is better connected to human destiny. The soul of a people is eternal because of war. Generative desire is rekindled by it like a torch in a wind that strives to put it out. Only the threat of death perpetuates earthly forms, only death makes the world divine. If children are not begotten in the white core of a crystal because of the illusion of eternity, the wombs of women are fecund because they are mortal. The gigantic monsters that roared before the adamite cavern and threatened all living beings perished because the desire in them froze. Because they were full of power and dominion, they were free from death's terror, and no voice in nature could warn them that they were not eternal. Death is the divine causality of the world. And the mystical initiation of this ancient truth is revealed through war! That blind generative will that provoked heroes in ancient tragedy roars in battle.

Chapter XXXIV

THE INFANTRY ADVANCES in black waves; the ground trembles beneath the uniform step of iron-clad boots; there is a chorus of soaring voices:

— Onward! Onward! Onward!

A tremor runs through the trenches, and persists vibrantly in the clinking of bayonets. The Germans shout:

— Hurrah! Hurrah! Hurrah!

There are thousands of voices. The point of their helmets barely appears when the French crush them with grenades. The Germans fire repeatedly from the shelter of a trench that is collapsing and filled with the dead. Staying in step, they raise their rifles to their faces and shoot. Innumerable, lizard-like flames rip through the shadows. The wave of assailants, Zouaves and foreign legionnaires, penetrates the trench, and is greeted by a bestial roar. The grenades set straw beds and the capes of the dead on fire, and smoke and the smell of burned flesh serve as background for the clamour of the wounded. A German soldier, covered in flames, runs across the field, shouting. The fire, climbing stealthily through the back of the trench, intensifies and surges when hit by grenades, reflecting the points of helmets and iron bayonets and revealing the soldiers' faces, pale, splashed with blood, covered in mud, eyes sharp like knives. — Allied artillery bombards the field extending from the rear of the trench, and carpet shelling cuts off the way for reserves coming to reinforce the front line. Wounded Germans sit up pleading:

— Frenchmen! Frenchmen! Comrades!

The uninjured throw down their rifles and raise their arms.

— Comrades! Comrades!

They form sombre groups, astonished, with the grim expression of abandonment. Defeat stupefies and debases them:

— We are not Prussians! We are Bavarians!

And another group, kneeling in mud, with their arms up:

— We Bavarians didn't want the war! Frenchmen! Frenchmen! Comrades!

Having lost any hope of victory, blind with a naïve and brutal instinct, they are like dispirited oxen. The French grant quarter with the proud expression of the victorious.

Chapter XXXV

ENGLISH TROOPS ATTACK from the left of the Ancre. Hundreds of cannon thundering at the same time open their red throats in the dawn's haze, and an arc of light trembles over the land. The bombardment, as dominant and tenacious as the soul of old England, has lasted three days. The soldiers stationed in the rearguard sleep heavily, in oblivion's stupor, and, when the hour arrives, the sergeant's whistle awakens them: They get up with herdlike rumbling, their eyes full of visions: Before leaving, they drink a cup of hot coffee, surrounded by baggage, rifles on their shoulders, packs on their backs. With uniform step, they move down the roadways in columns of four; their wet caps emit an acrid odour, and, shortly after the march begins, no one speaks. The journey seems interminable for the soldier when he walks thus, confined to a row, continuously seeing the back of the one who marches ahead, feeling water that runs off his helmet dripping down his skin. He wants to get to the battle, to hold tightly in his hands the rifle sleeping on his pained shoulder, to feel it warm and throbbing as though alive. The monotonous rhythm of his steps produces dizzying anguish: Toc! Toc! Toc!

Chapter XXXVI

UNDER THE SHELTER of mist and darkness, German troops abandon trenches that are collapsed and crushed by enemy artillery. They begin a stealthy retreat, but even when disguised by artillery fire in other sectors, English patrols on high alert discover the manoeuvre. Cannon lengthen their shots and begin bombardment of the second line. Searchlights illuminate the field, and a squadron of aeroplanes passes through the cloudy, dawn sky. Germans stretch out on the ground, under siege in a curtain of fire; planes locate them, and grenades begin to fall. Amidst clouds of smoke and turned-up earth, destroyed bodies fly: Arms torn from shoulders, black legs resembling hooks, pointed helmets holding heads by their chin straps, guts that fall over the living, covering them with blood and filth. The Germans, realizing their defeat, begin to shout:

— Englishmen! Englishmen! Pity! Have pity, we are men!

It is a frightened roar, like that of bulls in a pasture during an eclipse of the sun. The battle's resplendence trembles continuously over the horizon, and the artillery's thunder seems like a voice that emerges from the chasms of the earth.

Chapter XXXVII

ARRANGED in well-formed squadrons, the Indian Cavalry waits behind the line of attack; a shudder runs through it; spurs and sabres knock together. Horses perk up their ears, open their noses to the wind; some rear up and one runs through the battle bouncing its rider back and forth in the saddle. In the dawn's half-light, turbans whiten and silhouettes full of military harmony move like figures on a frieze. The stars grow pale, and the red splendour of fire rises on the horizon. At this moment the Indian Cavalry charges, unleashed, to take prisoners. Horses gallop and shake the land with a vast rumbling filled with ancient memories. Horsemen run with sabres high, eyes burning, mouths trembling in a smile that shows white teeth. The Germans, seeing them arrive, raise their arms:

— Mercy! Mercy!

The Indian horsemen pass by, stabbing them, and turn their horses, always with their sabres in the air. The curved blades flash ferociously over their turbans. A shout of surprise and anger pours forth:

— They aren't giving quarter! They aren't giving quarter!

Gripping their rifles, the Germans retreat; they watch the horsemen arrive amidst clouds of smoke and, taking refuge in hollows created by grenades, they open fire. Horses rear and run through the field with a long whinny, lips pounding, eyes facing front, manes raised. One frightened horse gallops with loosened reins, dragging from its hind-quarters a fallen horseman who has lost his turban, his long, black hair flowing like a crow's wing and blood bubbling on his chest. The Germans, between shots, raise a terrible cry:

— Death to England!

The Indian horsemen turn their horses and cruelly smile beneath the gleam of their sabres. They make one last gallop through the field of death and return to their camp.

Chapter XXXVIII

THE GENERAL HEADQUARTERS of Sir Francis Murray, veteran of the co-lonial wars, is in a neoclassical palace in the depths of Picardy. News from the battle arrives continuously. Along the great avenue of poplars pass automobiles for the Chiefs of Staff. Orderlies speak with soldier-cyclists who, ready to leave, wait at the foot of the stairs. Telephones ring in ex-pansive rooms that are muted and deserted. Four officers work in the library, its wall covered with military maps, and a meeting between two generals ends in the room next to it. They appear in the door to the library with lit Havanas and jovial smiles. The older has a large, grey moustache and clear, childlike blue eyes that are cloudy under his eye-brows. His great, white forehead contrasts with tanned cheeks full of wrinkles. The other is tall, strong, fiery, with gold glasses and an im-perious expression on his cleanly shaven face. The old man questions:

— Is there news from the French?

One of the officers searches through the papers in front of him, and hands him one:

— Here is the communiqué, my General.

— Good! What does it say?

— They have taken six thousand prisoners since yesterday.

The younger general interrupts:

— We haven't taken any... We haven't taken prisoners in many days.

The officers looked at each other, and one ventured:[20]

— Nonetheless, we have had great successes yesterday and today.

General Murray agreed with a nod:

— But without prisoners.

Sir William Scott, the older general, laughed with a worn-out laugh at the same time that he poured a glass of whisky:

— Without prisoners! Is it not true, gentlemen, that dispatches with-out prisoners aren't very impressive?

Sir Francis Murray looked at him as one looks at a child:

— Let's leave the theatrics to the Germans. Our dispatches are English dispatches. We haven't taken prisoners for many days because we must

---

20 Past tense is introduced here in the original and continues to the end of the chapter.

punish the crimes of Prussians who shouted surrender and then attacked our trenches with hand grenades without fear of reprisal, certain that the English would not fire against an enemy who turns himself in.

Sir Francis Murray spoke slowly, with a show of disgust. One of the officers asked:

— General, how much longer will the order to take no prisoners last?

— It must last until the end. The German Empire has broken its pacts, has broken the laws of war, has broken all traditions of International Law... But in this instance it is soldiers who forgot and disgraced military honour like savages, and we must impose on them the punishment imposed by us many times in Africa and Australia.

The telephone rang and one of the officers got up. All were quiet in the library. The dawn's light shone through the shutters of the windows and the lights flickered: A trace of fatigue was visible in each face. The officer who answered the telephone appeared in the doorway:

— Our advance is confirmed. A great victory and without prisoners!

Chapter XXXIX

AT THE APEX of night and day, a fine mist settles over the frozen Catalaunian Plains.[21] The army's mass is outlined against the mist. Cannon roll and horses gallop with a sonorous sound diffused through the great plain hardened by ice and bordered by blue-grey forests in the distance. Command officers prance about on their horses as they stop in front of battalions, lined up under unfurled flags. General Gouraud reviews the troops[22] and decorates flags with the Legion of Honour. He has an amputated arm and a face hardened by the sun, an exalted and mystic look, full of the blue light of sacred audacity. He kisses the flags as he puts the cross on them, and the flags, torn by enemy fire, flutter in tatters over the mutilated figure of the General. The tattered flags and that one-armed soldier damaged by the war form a unified and exemplary emotion. Bugles sound clearly, the cavalry parades at a gallop, cannon salute, and squads of infantrymen advance to the sound of drums. A religious emotion covers the great plain, and ancient shadows offer their laurels to the young heroes of divine France.

21 The Catalaunian Plains are the site of a fifth-century battle between the Romans and the forces of Atilla the Hun. Here the narrator refers to action that takes place on the plains near Châlons.
22 The name of the general, Henri Gouraud, appears as 'Goureaud' in the original and is corrected here.

Chapter XL

THERE ARE GREAT ENCAMPMENTS at Ypres and Arras, Verdun and
Reims, Thann and Metzeral. Along the roadways, under mutilated trees,
in the doors of taverns, in farm stables, every space surrounding these
heroic cities is full of soldiers. Cavalry patrols gallop along roadways
and cross sleeping hamlets with an intense and resounding racket. At
the edge of forests, soldiers, naked above the waist, sacrifice cows and
steers. Dead cattle hang from strong branches, and those about to die
make a commotion, frightened, jerking their halters. Hospital boats
move through green and cloudy rivers. They dock in backwaters to
bury the dead, and sail again, sounding their bells. In front of lodgings, groups of soldiers clean their firearms, brush down their horses,
prepare the teams, and load munitions onto wagons. Squads of foot soldiers bivouac at the edge of forests. Some bathe in the streams: Others
smoke their black pipes in the doorways of hostels, among wagons and
teams, while strong Friesian horses, their noses buried in rucksacks,
their necks bowed down, grind oat fodder. Convoys roll in the dawn's
mist, slowly, with a heavy swaying. The rigid form of cannon is outlined
under dirty tarps, and to the left rides a veteran soldier, with a red moustache waxed into two parts and the eyes of a villager, clear eyes accus-
tomed to looking far away, like those of a sailor but less sharp and more
full of the love of things. Large convoys roll along all the roads that lead
to the battle-front, and wagons are covered with branches to hide them
from the scrutiny of enemy planes: They file by, leaving wide tyre tracks,
and their guards, spread out on either side, march in silence. Green carriages with machine guns clatter alongside those carrying heavy, lead-
coloured boxes of munitions. To the rear of the trenches are flattened
forests burned by suffocating gasses, sacked farms, villages in rubble,
churches with their bell towers cut off... It is a succession of desolate
images, uninterrupted from the north coast to the Alsatian Mountains.
In the atriums of old cities grenades burst, stones fall from cathedrals,
porticos crowned by saints tremble in their foundations, rose windows
break and frightened swallows fly through deserted naves. In the light
of the new day, the land, mutilated by war, has a pained expression,
intense and terrible.

BIBLIOGRAPHY

Primary Texts

Valle-Inclán, Ramón del, *Autumn and Winter Sonatas: The Memoirs of the Marquis of Bradomín*, trans. by Margaret Jull Costa (Dedalus, 1998)

—— *Con el alba: el cuaderno de Francia (1916). Manuscrito inédito de Ramón del Valle Inclán*, ed. by Margarita Santos Zas, facsimile edn (Universidade de Santiago de Compostela, 2016)

—— *La lámpara maravillosa: ejercicios espirituales*, ed. by Francisco Javier Blasco Pascual (Espasa Calpe, 1995)

—— *La media noche: visión estelar de un momento de guerra* (Imprenta Clásica Española, 1917)

—— *The Lamp of Marvels: Aesthetic Meditations*, trans. by Robert Lima (Lindisfarne Press, 1986)

—— 'Midnight: *Astral Vision of a Moment of War* (excerpts)', trans. by Elizabeth Drumm, *PMLA*, 136.3 (2021), pp. 401–16

—— *Obras completas*, ed. by Margarita Santos Zas and others, 5 vols (Fundación José Antonio de Castro, 2018)

—— *Savage Comedies*, trans. by Christopher Colbath and Luis M. González, MHRA New Translations, 15 (Modern Humanities Research Association, 2022)

—— *Spring and Summer Sonatas: The Memoirs of the Marquis of Bradomín*, trans. by Margaret Jull Costa (Dedalus, 2013)

—— *Tyrant Banderas*, trans. by Peter Bush (New York Review Books, 2012)

—— *Un día de guerra (visión estelar) — La media noche: visión estelar de un momento de guerra*, ed. by Bénédicte Vauthier and Margartia Santos Zas, 3 vols (Universidade de Santiago de Compostela, 2017)

Secondary Texts

Bellini, Emiliano, 'El recuerdo almacenado: estética del recuerdo en Valle-Inclán y Proust', *Rivista di Filologia e Letterature Ispaniche*, 6 (2003), pp. 349–56

Bergson, Henri, *The Meaning of the War: Life and Matter in Conflict*, ed. by H. Wilden Carr (T. Fisher Unwin, 1915)

Berman, Jessica Schiff, *Modernist Commitments: Ethics, Politics, and Transnational Modernism* (Columbia University Press, 2011)

Bretz, Mary Lee, *Encounters Across Borders: The Changing Visions of Spanish Modernism, 1890–1930* (Bucknell University Press, 2001)

Cardona, Rodolfo, 'El tiempo de la *Sonata de otoño*', in *Ramón de Valle-Inclán: An Appraisal of His Life and Works*, ed. by Anthony N. Zahareas (Las Américas, 1986), pp. 216–23

Dougherty, Dru, 'Valle-Inclán, corresponsal de guerra: *La media noche*', in *Literatura hispánica y prensa periódica (1875–1931): actas del Congreso Internacional, Lugo, 25–28 de noviembre de 2008*, ed. by Javier Serrano Alonso and Amparo de Juan Bolufer (Universidade de Santiago de Compostela, 2009), pp. 565–85

—— *Un Valle-Inclán olvidado: entrevistas y conferencias* (Fundamentos, 1983)

Drumm, Elizabeth, 'La estética del recuerdo en *La lámpara maravillosa*: el proceso de pensar el tiempo', in *Valle-Inclán y las artes: congreso internacional, Santiago de Compostela, 25–28 de octubre de 2011*, ed. by Margarita Santos Zas, Javier Serrano, and Amparo de Juan Bolufer (Universidade de Santiago de Compostela, 2012), pp. 303–20

—— 'Henri Bergson on Time, Perception and Memory and Ramón del Valle-Inclán's *La lámpara maravillosa*', *Anales de la literatura española contemporánea*, 40.3 (2015), pp. 19–42

Fraser, Benjamin, *Encounters with Bergson(ism) in Spain: Reconciling Philosophy, Literature, Film and Urban Space* (University of North Carolina Department of Romance Languages, 2010)

Garlitz, Virginia, *El centro del círculo: 'La lámpara maravillosa' de Valle-Inclán* (Santiago de Compostela. Universidade de Santiago de Compostela, 2007)

—— 'La estética de Valle-Inclán en "La media noche" y "En la luz del día"', *Revista de estudios hispánicos*, 16 (1989), pp. 21–30

—— 'El ocultismo finisecular en Valle-Inclán', *El Pasajero*, 22 (2013) <https://www.elpasajero.com/ventolera/garlitzoccultismesp.html> [accessed 5 June 2023]

—— 'Valle-Inclán en la gira americana de 1910', in *Valle-Inclán, 1898–1998: escenarios: seminario internacional, Universidade de Santiago de Compostela, noviembre–diciembre, 1998*, ed. by Margarita Santos Zas and others (Universidade de Santiago de Compostela, 2000), pp. 91–122

Guerlac, Suzanne, *Thinking in Time: An Introduction to Henri Bergson* (Cornell University Press, 2006)

—— 'Thinking in Time: Henri Bergson (an Interdisciplinary Conference)', *MLN*, 120.5 (2005), pp. 1091–98

Jones, Donna V., 'Mysticism and War: Reflections on Bergson and His Reception during World War I', *Journal of French and Francophone Philosophy*, 24.2 (2016), pp. 10–20

Juan Bolufer, Amparo de, *La técnica narrativa en Valle-Inclán* (Universidade de Santiago de Compostela, 2000)

Lavaud, Eliane, 'Valle-Inclán y la Exposición de Bellas Artes de 1908', *Papeles de Son Armadans*, 81 (1976), pp. 115–28

Lavaud, Jean-Marie, 'Une collaboration de Valle-Inclán au journal *Nuevo Mundo* et l'exposition de 1912', *Bulletin Hispanique*, 71 (1969), pp. 286–311

López-Casanova, Arcadio, 'Valle-Inclán en Francia: "Un día de guerra"', *Valle Inclán (1898–1998): escenarios: seminario internacional Universidade de Santiago de Compostela, noviembre–diciembre, 1998*, ed. by Margarita Santos Zas (Universidade de Santiago de Compostela, 2000), pp. 159–78

Mascato Rey, Rosario, 'Tras la huella de Bergson: fundamentos para un estudio del intuicionismo en Valle-Inclán', *Anales de la literatura española contemporánea*, 34.3 (2009), pp. 67–94

Morón Aroroyo, Ciriaco, '*La lámpara maravillosa* y la ecuación estética', in *Valle-Inclán: An Appraisal of His Life and Works*, ed. by Anthony N. Zahareas (Las Américas, 1968), pp. 443–59

Pereiro Otero, José Manuel, *La escritura modernista de Valle-Inclán: orgía de colores* (Verbum, 2008)

Rogers, Gayle, 'Jiménez, Modernism/o, and the Languages of Comparative Modernist Studies', *Comparative Literature*, 66.1 (2014), pp. 127–47

—— *Modernism and the New Spain: Britain, Cosmopolitan Europe, and Literary History* (Oxford University Press, 2012)

Salaün, Serge, 'Valle-Inclán y la pintura', *Hecho teatral: revista de teoría y práctica del teatro hispánico*, 1 (2001), pp. 115–35

Santos Zas, Margarita, 'Introducción a la vida y obra de Valle-Incán', in *Cátedra Valle-Inclán*, ed. by Margarita Santos Zas and others (Centro de Humanidades Digitales de la Universidad de Alicante, 2008) <https://www.cervantesvirtual.com/portales/catedra_valle_inclan/vida_primeras_publicaciones> [accessed 10 March 2025]

——— 'Presentacion', in *Cátedra Valle-Inclán*, ed. by Margarita Santos Zas and others (Centro de Humanidades Digitales de la Universidad de Alicante, 2008) <https://www.cervantesvirtual.com/portales/cate­dra_valle_inclan/presentacion> [accessed 12 December 2024]

——— 'Valle-Inclán, contertulio: el nuevo café de levante', *Insula: revista de letras y ciencias humanas*, 738 (2008), pp. 13–15

——— 'Valle-Inclán en francés: expectativas e realidades', in *Outros verbos, novas lecturas: Valle-Inclán traducido (1906–1936)*, ed. by Rosario Mascato Rey (Consello da Cultura Galega, 2014), pp. 27–38

Santos Zas, Margarita, and others (eds), *Cátedra Valle-Inclán* (Centro de Humanidades Digitales de la Universidad de Alicante, 2008) <https://www.cervantesvirtual.com/portales/catedra_valle_inclan> [accessed 5 June 2023]

——— *Todo Valle-Inclán en Roma (1933–1936): edición, anotación, indices, facsimiles* (Universidade de Santiago de Compostela, 2010)

Soufas, C. Christopher, Jr, 'Spain', in *The Cambridge Companion to European Modernism*, ed. by Pericles Lewis (Cambridge University Press, 2011), pp. 151–69

——— *The Subject in Question: Early Contemporary Spanish Literature and Modernism* (Catholic University of America Press, 2007)

Vauthier, Bénédicte, and Margarita Santos Zas, 'Estudio y dossier genético', in Ramón del Valle-Inclán, *Un día de guerra (visión estelar) — La media noche: visión estelar de un momento de guerra*, ed. by Bénédicte Vauthier and Margartia Santos Zas, 3 vols (Universidade de Santiago de Compostela, 2017), III, pp. 19–35, 89–159

Vílchez Ruiz, Carmen E., 'De las ideas estéticas de Valle-Inclán en la prensa periódica (1902–1916): armonía de contrarios', in *Literatura hispánica y prensa periódica (1875–1931): actas del Congreso Internacional, Lugo, 25–28 de noviembre 2008*, ed. by Javier Serrano Alonso and Amparo de Juan Bolufer (Universidade de Santiago de Compostela, 2009), pp. 637–48

'La estética vallcinclániana a la luz de *La lámpara maravillosa*', *Elvira: revista de estudios filológicos*, 10 (2005), pp. 89–116

——— 'Las fuentes y conceptos teosóficos de La lámpara maravillosa a la luz de los autógrafos conservados en el legado Valle-Inclán Alsina', *Anales de la literature española contemporánea*, 41.3 (2016), pp. 725–50

——— 'Mística y cannabis como vía estética en Valle-Inclán: *La lámpara maravillosa*', in *Sobremesas literarias: en torno a la gastronomía en las letras hispánicas*, ed. by Laura Peña Garcia and Jesús Murillo Sagredo (Biblioteca Nueva, 2015), pp. 411–20

Vílchez Ruiz, Carmen E., and others (eds), *Archivo digital Valle-Inclán (1888–1936)* (Universidade de Santiago de Compostela, 2018) <http://www.archivodigitalvalleinclan.es> [accessed 12 December 2024]

Villanueva, Darío, '*La media noche* de Valle-Inclán: análisis y suerte de su técnica narrativa', in *Suma Valleinclaniana*, ed. by John P. Gabriele (Anthropos, 1992), pp. 415–44

—— *Valle-Inclán, novelista del modernism* (Editorial Tirant lo Blanch, 2005)

MHRA NEW TRANSLATIONS

A Selection of Recently Published Titles

Carl Sternheim, *A Chronicle of the Early Twentieth Century*
Translated by Fred Bridgham

Pablo Messiez, *The Eyes: A Telluric Melodrama*
Translated by Alma Prelec and María Bastianes

Ramón María del Valle Inclán, *Savage Comedies*
Translated by Christopher Colbath and Luis M. González

Michel-Jean Sedaine, *Le Philosophe sans le savoir*
Translated by Derek Connon

In Defence of Women
Translated by Joanna M. Barker

Hugo van Hofmannsthal, *The Incorruptible Servant*
Translated by Alexander Stillmark

Goethe, *The Natural Daughter* & Schiller, *The Bride of Messina*
Translated by F. J. Lamport

texts.mhra.org.uk

To sign up to the series mailing list,
email newtranslations@mhra.org.uk

The MHRA encourages and promotes advanced study and research in the field of the modern humanities, especially modern European languages and literature, including English, and also cinema. It aims to break down the barriers between scholars working in different disciplines and to maintain the unity of humanistic scholarship. The Association fulfils this purpose through the publication of journals, bibliographies, monographs, critical editions, and the MHRA *Style Guide*, and by making grants in support of research. Membership is open to all who work in the humanities, whether independent or in a university post, and the participation of younger colleagues entering the field is especially welcomed.

ALSO PUBLISHED BY THE ASSOCIATION

Tudor & Stuart Translations • European Translations
Critical Texts
Library of Medieval Welsh Literature • Jewelled Tortoise

Legenda

The Annual Bibliography of English Language & Literature

Austrian Studies
Modern Language Review
Portuguese Studies
The Slavonic & East European Review
Working Papers in the Humanities
The Yearbook of English Studies

www.mhra.org.uk

www.ingramcontent.com/pod-product-compliance
Lightning Source LLC
Chambersburg PA
CBHW030908050726
47500CB00009B/1295